AMAZING GRACE

LOST SOULS & BROKEN HEARTS #1

MICHELE BARDSLEY

ACKNOWLEDGMENTS

My deepest thanks to Robyn Peterman who created a world made of Magic & Mayhem where I originally brought Witches Gone Wild to life.

Using the bones of those previous adventures, I've built a new paranormal refuge in Lost Souls, Arkansas. This sanctuary is much like the one created by the citizens of Broken Heart, Oklahoma. Only with a magical tree and bear shifter guardian and this dude from the underworld.

And now, dear readers...

Welcome to the new world of Lost Souls & Broken Hearts.

CHAPTER 1

Broken Heart, Oklahoma

itch Grace Anne Hobbs stroked the bumpy, colorful back of her beloved familiar to keep her calm, not that Elizardbeth AKA Liz needed any extra Zen. Since getting sick a couple of days ago, her familiar didn't have enough energy to do more than droop across Grace's legs like a bouquet of wilted flowers.

The small lobby at the vet's office was painted in soothing blues and greens with white straight back wooden chairs and little matching tables that held copies of *National Geographic, Broken Heart Banner,* and *Animal Wellness.* Grace also saw a copy of Theodosia Monroe's *The Care and Feeding of Dragons.*

Sitting next to Grace was the last person she ever expected to share space with—the violet-haired fairy named Zerina. Even in a town like Broken Heart, Oklahoma where most everyone belonged to parakind, Zerina stuck out. The fairy was dressed in a lavender corset, black leather mini-skirt, and shiny purple boots with black laces that traversed from the ankle to the knee. The outfit was as intimidating as the woman wearing it. Even though Zerina was known for being short-tempered and verbally blunt, Grace couldn't help but admire the fairy's confidence and don't-give-a-crap attitude.

If only I had a tenth of Zerina's bad-assery, she thought.

As a witch who specialized in plant life, Grace spent most of her time fabricating hybrids that held both beauty and magic. Parakind from all over the world ordered her ointments, tonics, and creams. It was a satisfying life, even if it was a lonely one. Grace rarely ventured into town, and she never asked for help, but not a single poultice or tincture Grace had given to Liz made the familiar feel better. Desperation had pushed her to seek out Broken Heart's only veterinarian and get the stranger's advice.

"Okay. I give up. What happened to your baby dragon?" Zerina's face scrunched as she peered at Liz, poking the lizard on the head with one manicured nail. Little purple skulls dotted the black nail polish. "Did she fall into a pit of acid, or what?" Zerina's accent was lyrical and straight from the Emerald Isle. "This thing is crazy looking."

The fairy's observations smacked of the pot calling the kettle rainbow. After all, a small green rabbit with long diamond-bedazzled ears sat on Zerina's shoulder. The tiny thing was asleep; its furry head snuggled against the fairy's neck. Zerina saw the direction of Grace's gaze and affectionately tugged on one of her bunny's ears. "This is a púca. His name is Kevin."

Kevin popped open one golden eye and peered at Grace. "That means handsome in Gaelic, you know," he said in a soft Irish lilt. With that information delivered, he closed his eye. Then he began to snore.

"Oh," said Grace. "He's nice." She looked at Zerina and gave her a polite smile. "This is Liz. She's a *chlamydosaurus.*"

"Isn't that an STD?" Zerina snatched her hand back. "Didn't anyone ever tell her no glove, no love?"

Grace laughed. "Liz is a frilled-neck lizard, known as a *chlamydosaurus kingii*." Liz was forest green with a stripe of deep red across her spine. When she got excited, horny, territorial, or just because she felt like it, she'd show off her orange and red frill. It made her head appear as if it was stuck in an opened umbrella. "So, not a baby dragon. She's a full-grown lizard. My familiar."

"A witch, huh? No shit." The fae's amethyst gaze moved from Liz to Grace. "By the way, I'm Zerina. You're new around here, aren't you?"

"Yes. My name is Grace Hobbs." She'd moved to the protected paranormal community less than three months ago. She stayed mostly to herself, hiding away in a little trailer on the outskirts of Broken Heart proper, near the burned-out husk of the old Thrifty Sip convenience store. It put her close to the edge of the town's Invisi-Shield—a magic-tech force field that protected the residents from the outside world. Anyone without permission AKA a tattoo "key" adhered to their skin could not enter the grounds. In addition, outsiders would only see flat, endless fields of dirt and debris. Humans avoided the area, believing Broken Heart BC (Before Consortium) had been blown up in a severe gas leak that still affected most of the area.

It wasn't so much that Grace needed the protection for herself, but rather, protection for those who got within three feet of her. Grace's self-enforced seclusion wasn't because she was anti-social. On the contrary, she missed being around other people.

No, Grace was definitely not anti-social.

She was cursed.

Wow. I've seen better hair on a scarecrow that's been through a tornado and set on fire. And what in the blazes is that color? It looks like unicorn shit.

Grace side-eyed the curse...the ghost of Dorcas Hoar. Her ancestor's nemesis. Her unwanted companion. Her family burden. Other than Liz, no one, not even the ghost-whispering vampires of the Family Amahté, could see the pain-in-the-ass who haunted her every waking moment. This asinine spirit even followed her into the bathroom. You know what? It was really hard to poop with a smartass crone broadcasting a play-by-play.

She watched Dorcas zoom upward, perform a perfect triple Lutz, and land tippy-toe on Zerina's head. She looked at Grace, grinned, and then bowed. *Thank you, thank you.*

Oh, gawd. On the rare occasions Grace went into town, Dorcas did her level best to annoy Grace to the point where she snapped and yelled at the ghost—or, as other people saw it—a crazy witch inexplicably yelling at thin air. If her efforts to irritate failed, Dorcas would do everything possible to make her laugh. Grace couldn't imagine that her sudden cackling for no apparent reason was any less disturbing than watching her scream, "Shut up, already!" to no one.

It wasn't like Dorcas had stayed the same Puritan witch in death that she had been in life. Today, the crazy old bat wore her gray hair in double-ponytails and a 1960s ensemble straight out *Barbarella*. Fashion in 1665 Salem had been limited to scratchy dresses designed to cover every inch of a woman's body and sweat-inducing bonnets that invited bugs to nest in unwashed hair.

Dorcas was making rabbit ears behind Zerina's head. Then she pretended to give Zerina double wet willies. Grace pressed her lips together and gave a slight shake of her head. Dorcas took this as a challenge and proceeded to sit on Zerina's head and fart.

"Stop it," muttered Grace under her breath, trying to choke down her laughter. *Damn it, Dorcas.*

Zerina narrowed her gaze. "Stop what?"

Grace pretended innocence as she looked at Zerina. "What?"

Zerina's expression turned suspicious. "Are you talking to yourself?" She pursed her lips. "Do you have voices in your head? Maybe the crazy is contagious, and you infected your lizard."

Grace had long given up trying to explain Dorcas—even to paranormal beings who lived with the outrageous and the weird every day. Instead, she looked at Zerina and smiled. "You might be right."

Way to stand up for yourself, Grace. Where's your backbone? Did you leave it home with your fashion sense?

Grace wanted to point out that Dorcas wouldn't know fashion if Vera Wang bit her saggy ol' butt. But she couldn't respond to Dorcas's insult. Not if she didn't want to look crazier than she already did.

Dorcas went horizontal and started swimming around the waiting room. For a witch born in the 1600s, she had an impressive backstroke. *I'm bored. Put me out of my misery, and get a new familiar already. Maybe a cat. Back in my day, we didn't have fancy animal familiars like overgrown lizards.*

"Shut up, you old hag," said Liz as she shook herself awake and wobbled upright.

"Old hag!" Zerina's steely purple gaze affixed onto the lizard.

"Oh," said Grace, "she wasn't talking to you. That's uh, her nickname for me."

"Your nickname is Old Hag," said Zerina disbelievingly.

"Ever since I was knee-high to a grasshopper," lied Grace.

"Ugh. Grasshoppers. I did eat some of those." Liz dug her

tiny claws into Grace's jeans. "I don't feel so good." She made a strange guttural sound.

Before Grace could do much more than utter, "uh oh," Liz groaned, lurched forward, and puked.

On Zerina.

Mushed crickets, the aforementioned grasshoppers, and digested mealworms splattered the fairy's leather mini-skirt and boots. The noxious brew smelled worse than it looked, adding to the horror Grace felt as the fairy looked down at her ruined clothing.

Hahahahahahaha! Sweet Satan's Asshole. Dorcas grabbed her sides and swooshed around in a circle like laundry in the spin cycle. *That's hilarious. Hahahahahahaha!*

Grace glared at the ghost, but Dorcas didn't notice. The jerkface was too busy hyperventilating with laughter. She fell to the floor and rolled around, guffawing.

"I am so sorry," said Grace. Zerina's revenge tactics were legendary, and she could only imagine what kind of payback was in store for covering the fairy in a familiar's disgusting vomit. "Um...is Kevin okay?"

"Kevin," said Zerina, turning her stunned gaze onto Grace. "You want to know if the sleeping púca on my shoulder survived your STD lizard's vomit volcano?"

Grace grimaced. Shit. What a dumb question to ask. Kevin was fine. He hadn't moved a muscle despite the ruckus as if Zerina got puked on daily, and the fairy wasn't about to turn an innocent witch into...well, who knew with Zerina? Rumor had it that she'd once buried a vampire in a ton of pink glitter, and she'd purportedly *liked* him.

Horrified, Grace watched as Zerina plucked a teeny pink shoe from the mess clinging to the skirt.

"Onya, mate. Ta for the assist." Liz rose onto two legs balancing on Grace's lap as she held out a clawed hand. "That belongs to my Happy Birthday Harpy." Liz eyed the shoe. "That's a bit of mess, isn't it?"

"What did I tell you about eating shoes?" berated Grace as she grabbed the packet of Wet Wipes from her purse. No wonder Liz had been sick. She'd probably gotten the damn thing stuck in her intestines.

"You said not to eat *your* shoes." Liz's collar flared out and while Grace was glad to see her familiar getting her mojo back, she was less than thrilled that it had been at the expense of Zerina's clothing.

Zerina's expression was pure horror as she stared at Liz. "You murder shoes?"

"I only nibbled 'em a bit," groused Liz. "Grace can still wear 'em."

"Please tell me you only ate one of Happy Birthday Harpy's shoes," said Grace. The packet crinkled under her nervous grip as she took out a wipe and used it to pluck tiny plastic heel from Zerina's pinched fingers. She wrapped it up and then tucked it into the outer pocket of her handbag. She took out a second wipe and scrubbed Liz's face.

"Didn't like the taste of the first so I'd hardly eat the second," answered Liz. She flicked out her tongue. "Now my face tastes like bitters. I hate bitters."

All this time the two of you thought I'd be the one to get Grace killed, hooted Dorcas, *but it's gonna be you that does it, Liz. Look at that fairy's face! She's trying to decide if she'd rather make Grace implode or explode. Ahahahahaha!*

"I'll pay your cleaning bill," said Grace as she offered the entire package of Wet Wipes to Zerina. "Or buy you replacements. Just...well, let me know."

The fairy took the Wet Wipes, studied her skirt, and then turned her fiery purple gaze on Grace. She stared at Grace for so long, Grace nearly melted under the impact of that hot glare. In fact, she felt her scalp tingle and wondered if Zerina really was trying to make her explode.

"Miss Hobbs?" A pretty young woman wearing pink scrubs and staring at a chart stepped into the lobby. "We're ready for Elizardbeth," she said. It took the woman a moment to look up and take in the wretched scene—from Zerina's soiled clothing to Grace's chagrinned expression. "Is everything all right?"

"Fine," said Grace. "In fact, I think Liz is all better. We're gonna go." Grace tucked Liz under her arm, grabbed her purse, and offered one more "I'm so, so, sorry" to Zerina before she hurried out of the vet's office.

Grace made a beeline for her mint green and tan cruiser bicycle that she'd parked on the side of the brick building. She didn't drive motorized vehicles anymore because Dorcas's antics had turned Grace into a major road hazard. She'd gotten into more fender benders than she wanted to recount, so she'd traded in her car for something less lethal. The bike wasn't so bad. Attached to the handlebars was a basket, padded with a nice little memory foam cushion for Liz.

Grace shoved her purse and her familiar into the basket, flipped up the kickstand, and hopped onto the seat. No sense in tempting fate or Zerina by sticking around. She peddled as fast as she could toward home.

And all the while, Dorcas flew alongside her, pointing and laughing and laughing and laughing.

CHAPTER 2

Somewhere in the Arkansas Ozarks
Near White River

"Where does a bear shit in the woods?"

Tabor Standing Bear flipped the pancakes and then turned to look at his grandfather, Theobold Cotton, as old as dirt and as ornery as a bee-stung bear. His gray hair fell like a silver waterfall down his back and he was dressed like the 1960s and the 1970s had gotten drunk and slept together. Pops was nearly seven feet tall and 400 pounds— and that was in his human form. Pops was hella bigger when he shifted into a bear. Of course, most bear shifters were naturally big in both human and animal forms. That was part and parcel of being one of nature's beasts.

"Ha, ha, grandpa. That one never gets hold." Tabor scooped the pancakes off the frying pan and added them to the teetering stack near the stove. Their fluffy goodness emitted a honey-fried smell that had his mouth watering. "You know I have an actual working bathroom."

"Back in my day, we had to go out in the snow and walk

uphill both ways, to even get to the outhouse. And we didn't use no fancy toilet paper, either. Leaves, Tabor. That's nature's toilet paper."

"I'm pretty sure you were the one who built the bathroom in this cabin."

Pops grinned. "Only because your grandmother insisted."

Tabor knew the story well. Grandma Beth had told it many times at family get-togethers. Wasps had built a nest inside the dilapidated outhouse—one that had probably been around since the first bear shifter guardian built the cabin in 1693. She'd gone in to do her business and ended up being chased by the wasps from the outhouse, to the banks of the White River, where she jumped into the water and ruined her favorite dress.

Pops had started construction on the indoor water closet the same day his wife, dripping, cursing, and covered in wasp stings, had returned to the cabin and demanded, "A real bathroom, damn it!"

Tabor had inherited the cabin along with the Standing Bear duty to protect the *Franklinia Magica* that had been planted more than three centuries ago. A renewable source of magic and now the only tree of its kind in North America, it had once brought together both humans and parakind to live in harmony. The area had once been populated by a thriving community, but now only Tabor's family cabin and a few crumbling buildings remained of the abandoned town. The place had been desolate for so long it no longer had a name, much less a footnote in the Arkansas history books.

Pops edged behind him to rummage in the fridge. His grandfather was visiting for the next few days, and Tabor was glad for the company. But the kitchen wasn't exactly large, and with two bear shifters crammed into it, the space felt even smaller than usual. With the exception of whipping up easy breakfast foods, he was pretty much useless as a cook. It was why he spent very little time in the kitchen—only microwaving the occasional meal—and shifting into his bear form to go eat nature's bounty. Unfortunately, his grandfather wasn't as young as he used to be, and shifting could take a toll on the elderly—hence, the breakfast-for-dinner Tabor was cooking for Pops and himself.

"So, how's the ol' love life, Tabor? You found anyone giving you the honey jitters?" Pops threw a grin over his shoulder. "My Beth smelled like the best batch of Manuka honey ever made. Every Standing Bear who's fallen in true love had that first sweet scent of honey—that's when you know you've met your mate."

"Pops, I haven't dated in a while. I live in the back of beyond." None of the women he'd ever dated had given him the honey jitters. Every Standing Bear couple had a honey-scent-fated-mate anecdote, but he'd wondered for several years now if those stories were just Standing Bear tall tales. "Besides, I'm too old to believe in fairytales about fated love."

"It's not a fairytale," Pop insisted.

Tabor grunted as he turned off the gas flame, ignoring the look of consternation on Pop's face. He pushed the frying pan back to a cool burner and put the spatula onto the spoon rest. He grabbed the plate of stacked pancakes and walked to the breakfast nook, sliding the plate onto the table between the massive bowl of cut fruit and a pile of bacon that rivaled the Great Pyramid in height.

"Let's eat," Tabor said. He gestured to the table of food. "The only true love I'm going to find right now is this plate of bacon."

"You're too cynical, boy," said Pops.

"Not about eating." Tabor couldn't wait to get his paws on the bacon and pancakes. He looked at the massive jar of honey with a waxy comb soaked in the amber liquid and felt his stomach rumble. Nothing was better in the world than being able to drown his food in syrupy nirvana.

"Pops?" He looked over his shoulder. His grandfather held two glasses in one hand and carton of orange juice in the other, but his gaze was trained on the large picture window above the kitchen sink. The sun hadn't quite set, so the sky was an orange-ish purple melting into indigo. His wrinkled face held an expression of amazement.

"What have you been feeding those rabbits?" he asked.

"What rabbits?"

Tabor joined his grandfather at the window and looked outside. It was his habit to leave on the back porch light until he went to bed, but even if the light hadn't been on, he would've seen the multitude of rabbits spilling out of the tree line and into the entire yard. These bunnies were not cute or fluffy or, you know, *alive*. In various stages of decomposition, the bunnies bumped and twisted against each other, growling and gnashing their long teeth as they pushed against the cabin.

"So," said Pops. "Looks like you've got a zombie rabbit infestation." He looked at Tabor. "You might want to do something about that."

～

*L*ucas Dark studied at the broken weathered wooden steps that led into the abandoned church. Before time and nature had reclaimed it, the chapel had been a quaint white clapboard building with a cheerful bronze-topped steeple and a dark green roof. Though the steeple no longer housed a bell, the two beautiful stained glass front windows remained intact.

Dirt and ivy partially covered the panes, but he could make out the images. On the left window he saw a multi-trunked tree with winding branches filled with red leaves and white blooms. That tree was known as the *Franklinia Magica*. His gaze switched to the other window and he studied the raven-haired woman who wore a crown of white flowers and a purple robe. Her name was Deliverance Hobbs. Next to her stood a grizzly bear on its hind legs—a long ago shifter ancestor of the Osage Bear Clan. The image depicted the witch and the shifter with hands and paws reaching above their heads where a gold pentagram hovered. At the talisman's center was a tear-shaped obsidian stone.

"*Sol niger cantatis,*" he whispered. The enchanted black sun, a talisman created in 1693 by the last Salem witch coven. To protect themselves from the witch trials, they removed all the magic from those who lived in Salem and housed it inside the amulet. And in the amulet, a single seed from a long dead species that, once planted, would bloom and prosper—and give the magic to a new, more deserving town and its citizens.

Apparently, the plan hadn't exactly worked out exactly as the coven had planned. As the sun kissed the edge of the night sky, the crickets chirped, the bees buzzed, and the wind whispered against the long grasses and densely packed leaves of the surrounding trees. It was unfortunate that the town hadn't lasted very long and the people who'd once been a part of it were long gone. There was a wild beauty here, a magic that belonged to Mother Nature herself, outside of the bewitched 300-year-old tree housed within this decrepit little church.

Lucas shook his head. He was used to death. The death of people. He understood how souls carried their regrets with them into the afterlife. He'd grown up in the underworld, watching humans stumble onto the black shores of the River Styx, bewildered. Death didn't care if you were ready to leave the earthly plane. It didn't discriminate. It couldn't be bribed or reasoned with. It simply was.

The death of this town was so old it felt wrapped in cobwebs and rolled in dust. Not even ghosts lived here.

No one did.

Except for the bear guardian.

Him, he could deal with.

But first the tree.

Lucas climbed the rickety steps, his jeans catching on the splintered wood as he stepped onto the small porch. The door hung off its hinges and it screeched in protest as he pushed it inward. The musty smell of disuse and the fetid stench of rot clung to his nostrils as he stepped inside the church.

He stared at the overturned pews, the collapsed altar, and the crumbling walls. In the midst of the building, bursting through the floor and reaching toward the rickety roof with spindly, bare branches, was the source of ancient magic. The tree, even in its weakened state, was glorious.

Thirteen trunks no more than ten inches around each twisted together to form the tree's massive center. He lifted his gaze to the multitude of limbs, which should've been covered in dark red leaves and bright white flowers. Instead, they looked like the bony fingers of an old skeleton.

Something skittered from around the tree, hopped over his foot and tumbled out the door.

Lucas turned and watched the dead bunny spin down the stairs and, with one leg dragging behind it, hop in the direction of the guardian's cabin.

Damn it.

He jumped over the stairs and strode toward the fleeing rabbit, following it into the forest beyond.

❧

*T*abor had never seen any kind of zombie before, and frankly, it had never occurred to him that rabbits could be zombified. And now, there was a seething mass of little undead creatures trying to get into his house. "Where did they come from?"

"Oh, I ordered 'em from undeadrabbits.com," said Pops sarcastically. He put the glasses back into the cabinet and returned the orange juice to the fridge. "I don't freaking know. The hopping dead isn't my wheelhouse." He pulled his cell phone out of the back pocket of his faded jeans. "We need back-up."

Tabor watched his grandfather lean over the sink, open the window, and aim his cellphone camera at the dead bunnies. Here in the boonies, Internet was spotty at best, but a nearby cell tower insured the reliability of mobile phones. Good thing, too. Not that Tabor thought he'd ever need to call anyone about a zombie bunny attack.

"Holy shit. That one has two penises." The old man paused. "Oh. Never mind. Those are intestines."

"Gross." Tabor glanced at the food-laden table. "So much for breakfast."

Pops reared back, shrieking in a very un-bear-like way as one of the rabbits hopped onto the sill. Its eyes were red, and its mouth filled with bloody razor-sharp teeth. It fell into the copper farmhouse sink, growling and spitting as it scratched at the sides.

"For Goddess' sake, Pops. Shut the damn window!" Tabor yelled.

Pops slammed the window shut, but not before another zombunny stuck its little ratty head inside. The descending frame crushed it. "Crap on a cracker!" Pops blanched as he forced the window all the way down, ignoring the ick dripping off the sill. He quickly twisted the top two locks.

The snarling bunny in the sink jumped up, aiming its fetid bucked teeth at the old man's elbow. Pops screamed with the same enthusiasm one might find in a thirteen-year-old girl standing in the front row at a boy-band concert. He even did a windmill twirl that would make a backup dancer proud.

"Watch out!" Tabor took the still hot frying pan from the stove and smacked the damned thing's skull.

Its head cracked and flopped to the side, revealing neck muscles and white bone. The smell of burnt hair added to the disgusting smell of rotted meat. Tabor covered his mouth and nose with the back of his arm and watched the dead bunny hiss and growl as it tried to get free of its copper prison.

"Hit it again!" yelled Pops. "Hit it again!"

Tabor complied.

Again.

And again.

Until the zombunny was as flat as a used paper plate. It still moved, mostly in circles, but still. How did you kill something that was already dead?

"Shove it in the disposal," directed Pops.

"I'm not doing that," said Tabor. "It'll ruin the machine."

"Are you serious right now?"

"The disposal won't grind bone and fur, all right? It's meant for potato peels and apple cores."

The zombunny roared and leapt upward, a smelly, furry dead fucking rabbit pancake. Tabor smashed the creature onto the bottom of the sink, flipped the skillet and used its handle to shove the wiggling mass into the garbage disposal.

"What are you waiting for?" he yelled at his grandfather. "Turn on the disposal!"

Pops scurried around Tabor, leaned forward and flipped the switch near the faucet. The machine groaned a metallic protest as it ground the rabbit into pulp. Seconds later, the thing was finally gone.

"See," said Pops. "It totally grinds bone and fur."

"Fun-fucking-tastic." Tabor tossed the skillet into the sink with a hollow clang. "Well, I'm never using that pan again. Or the sink. Or the disposal."

"You'll have to replace everything," agreed Pops. He waved a hand under his nose. "Whew. That smells worse than roadkill fried in poop juice."

"Really?" asked Tabor. "Roadkill. In poop juice."

Pops grinned. "You've tried your grandmother's cooking. Am I wrong?"

"I'm telling her you said that."

"If you do, I'll tell her that you were the one who finished off last jar of Manuka honey."

Tabor flinched. "Okay, okay. Stalemate."

Thump. Thump. Thump.

"I think they're trying to break down the back door," said Tabor. He hurried to the door, locked it, and peeped out the side window. The bunnies had formed towers and were smacking themselves against the thick wood. He glanced at Pops. "I thought you were calling back-up?"

"Yep."

"But not grandma, right?"

"Are you kidding me? I'd sooner go outside and get eaten by those things than interrupt the sacred annual girls' trip to Las Vegas."

Two seconds after Pops sent a series of texts with pictures, a tall woman with the vibe of a warrior and the appearance of punk rocker magically popped into their kitchen. She was dressed in a black corset, a neon pink leather mini-skirt, and ballerina boots as black as her fairy's heart.

"Zerina." Tabor glared at his grandfather. "Really?"

CHAPTER 3

"*D*on't get your panties in a bunch, Tabor," said Zerina. "I promise not to send you to Mount Rainier. Again."

"Naked," said Tabor. "While I was in the shower."

"It was only for a couple of minutes."

"It felt like a couple of decades. Especially since you put me in the starting lane of one of the beginner trails." He glared at her. "In front of the Presbyterian Seattle Senior Ladies League."

"It's not like you died. Or they died."

"They tried to put me in their van! I had to wash off old lady drool. And phone numbers written in lipstick. On. My. Ass."

Zerina smirked. "That's what you get for eating all of the Manuka honey."

The Standing Bears had known Zerina for a couple of centuries. In the early 1800s she'd made friends with the Marchands, who were wolf shifters that had emigrated from France and lived near Vincennes in the Indiana Territory.

How or why an Irish fairy ended up in the middle of America was something she had never fully explained.

At the time, the shifter groups in North America were small and well known to each other. The Osage Bear Clan had traded with the werewolves in the Indiana territory, and thus Zerina had also become a friend to Arkansas's bear shifters.

These days, parakind lived together more peaceably than they did back in those days, especially with the vampires. Back then the Consortium, the parakind organization started by the vampires Patrick and Lorcan O'Halloran, was in early days in Europe and still building the considerable influence it had now in parakind communities. So, the undead in America tended to border on feral. *Deamhan fola.* Blood demons. *Deamhan fola* were the kind of vampires who didn't have souls and thought of humans as walking buffets.

The last person Tabor wanted to see on any day of the week was Zerina—much less on a hot August night while his home was being attacked by zombie rabbits. In a lot of ways, Zerina was a lot like the tormenting older sister Tabor never had or wanted. But Zerina had one redeemable quality.

"Where's Kevin?"

"At home sleeping. He had a checkup at the vet's this morning and he's decided to celebrate his good health by taking another damned nap. It's all he does." She put her hands on her hips and tapped her foot, her purple gaze zeroing in on Tabor's grandfather. "Why are you sending me pictures of rotting hares, Pops?" She paused. "Did that one rabbit have two penises?"

"Intestines," said Pops.

"Oh." Zerina marched to the kitchen window, pulled back the curtain, and took a long look. She whirled around and stabbed Tabor with a stony glare. "It's The Walking Dead: Rabbit Edition out there. What did you do, Tabor?"

"Me? I didn't do anything." He pointed to the abandoned meal cooling on the table. "I was making pancakes and minding my own damned business."

Zerina, who had an enviable cast-iron stomach, sauntered to the table and picked up a piece of crisp bacon. She took a bite then waved the slice around. "I don't do zombies. I got nothing."

"Well, we're not calling Beth," said Pops. "She and the girls are in Las Vegas."

"That time of year, huh?" Zerina nodded. "That leaves us with one option." She twirled a finger into the air.

Seconds later, a pale blonde woman wearing a red *Bloody Good Cook* apron over a blue T-shirt and jeans flickered into the kitchen. She was barefoot, holding a pair of barbecue tongs, and scowling at everyone. "What the fuck is going on?" she demanded. "I just put on the burgers, and I hate well done."

"Tabor and Theobold Standing Bear meet Patsy Marchand, Queen of the *Loup de Sang*—and apparently, the grill."

Patsy pointed the tongs at Zerina and clicked them together. Tabor harbored a tiny hope the vampire would pinch his fairy nemesis with them. "Maybe give the vampire queen more warning next time."

"We have an undead hare problem."

"Ha, ha. I never get tired of your jokes about my beautician past, Zee. You know I can zap you into the playroom with my kids, right? Remember last time?"

"I still have the bruises." Zerina winced then rolled her eyes and jabbed a thumb at the window over the kitchen sink. "Take a look, your highness."

Patsy stomped across the kitchen and peered through the window. "Holy crap. It's Dawn of the Dead Rabbits out there." She turned to Tabor. "How did you manage to summon a zombie bunny army?"

"I didn't," said Tabor. "Why does everyone think this is my fault? They just showed up."

"The only thing powerful enough around here to call forth this kind of crazy shit is Frank," said Pops.

"Who the hell is Frank?" asked Patsy. "And why didn't you call him?"

"Because Frank is an ancient magical tree called the *Franklinia Magica*," said Tabor. At Patsy's blank look, he decided to give a quick mini-history. "It's been here since 1693, when it was planted by Deliverance and Philip Hobbs —witch refugees from Salem. The tree has all the magic that once belonged to the Salem witches. The Osage Bear Clan agreed to be the guardians for the tree, and we've kept our end of that bargain for the last three-hundred years." Tabor looked at his grandfather. "At least, our family has." The rest of his clan had moved on as they lost faith in their calling. "It's never brought forth a zombie bunny army before."

"Well, it's been ailing, hasn't it?" Pops waved his hands. "Maybe this is the tree's call for help."

"Y'all have a magic tree that makes zombie rabbits?" Patsy put her hands on her hips. "Are you shitting me?"

"Irrelevant, and not why I brought you here, Pats. Everyone knows you're the zombie whisperer," said Zerina. She snagged another piece of bacon and dipped it in the honey jar. "So make with the whispering."

~

Broken Heart, Oklahoma

"I need me cricket popcorn!" yelled Liz. The familiar was curled onto the puffy blue couch, which reminded Grace of squashed blueberries, ready to watch her favorite TV program, *The Familiar Way*. Most humans were unaware that parakind had their own TV shows, including nighttime soap operas. You had to know how to tune in to the ParaNormal Network or PNN.

A swell of dramatic music filtered into the space. A sexy female voice said, "*Spellsworth. A town of independent familiars who ditched their witches centuries ago to live independent lives. But Spellsworth remains under the tiny thumbs of its founding family, the Hetterson clan, raccoon familiars who will stop at nothing to keep their power and add more wealth to their considerable coffers.*

"*In our last episode, Freda Hetterson, the youngest daughter, had left town with bad-boy chipmunk Hayes Mayfield. Abandoned by Hayes, Freda has returned home and given birth to twin sons. Meanwhile, the murder of Great Grandfather Elijah Hetterson, the most hated familiar in town, still goes unsolved.*

"*Will Freda keep her babies, or will she cave to the pressure of her family to put the twins up for adoption? And why are the Hettersons keeping evidence hidden from the detectives that might lead to their patriarch's killer? Find out now on...The Familiar Way.*"

Grace brought her familiar the freshly popped popcorn with crispy crickets and put it next to Liz. "You're welcome," she said.

"Yeah, yeah. Thanks, Grace. Now move your bum!"

Grace rolled her eyes and made her way into the back—and only—bedroom. She sat down at the dressing table, a long-ago garage-sale find that she hadn't wanted to give up when she moved to Broken Heart. Everything else, aside from her clothes, plants, and potions, had been replaceable.

She sat down and stared at her hair.

Her purple hair with sparkling gold streaks.

Prior to the run-in with Zerina, Grace had been a brunette. Plain brown hair that hadn't had a sparkle or gleam to it at all.

It's better than the neon green with pink streaks you had after breakfast, said Dorcas. *And the puke-yellow with orange chunks that appeared around lunchtime. It's been this way for hours—maybe the spell's almost done.*

Dorcas sounded like she was actually trying to make Grace feel better about her scary hair—even though the old bat had laughed at the original bright-white strands with black spiders that Zerina had given her right after the whole Liz vomit fiasco.

"I kinda like it," said Grace.

"Good. Because it's not going to change again unless I undo the spell."

Grace yelped and jumped up from her changing table. She turned to face the four people who'd suddenly appeared in her bedroom.

Holy shit, yelled Dorcas. *Give an old woman a heart attack!*

"You'd have to have a heart for that, you old hag," said Liz.

"Hush up," Grace said to both Liz and Dorcas. She recognized Zerina—now dressed in pink and black, but still wearing the same irritated expression she had this morning at the vet's office. Next to her was Patsy, the Queen of the *Loup de Sang* and basically Broken Heart's head honcho. Grace hadn't met Patsy face-to-face, but she hadn't expected the queen to be barefoot, wearing a barbecue apron, and holding tongs. The other two people were men the size of linebackers. One looked like he'd fallen out of the 1960s, and the other...

Broad shoulders. Narrow waist. Jeans that hugged muscular thighs. He wore a pair of black cowboy boots, a belt with a buckle the size of a plate, and a khaki short-sleeved shirt with pearl snap buttons. Underneath the tan cowboy hat was the most handsome face she'd ever seen. Those angular cheeks could cut glass, and his chin sported an adorable dent. His nose was slightly crooked, but the imperfection only enhanced his good looks. *What's wrong with you? Stop drooling in the direction of the hottie with the body. Relationships, even short-lived ones, are not in the cards. Not ever.*

Dorcas had ended her love life, which at the age of twenty-three, had consisted of two whole boyfriends. She'd broken up with Boyfriend #1 on her own because he kept putting his penis into other women. Boyfriend #2 hit the road after Grace appeared to lose her mind thanks to Dorcas constantly scaring the shit out of her. She screamed a lot during those first weeks with the ghost. The warlock might've been okay with that—witches weren't exactly known for their mental stability—but then Dorcas went all Donkey Kong on his ass. At the end, he believed Grace was trying to kill him, so he left without saying a word.

Grace blinked, and then noticed everyone in the room was staring at her. Including, Mr. Tall, Dark, and Beefcake. Oops. She'd gone off the hormonal rails there for a minute. Maybe the acid trip down memory lane was because she couldn't quite comprehend the turn her life had taken in the last thirty seconds.

"Hello." Zerina snapped her fingers. "Are you having a seizure?"

"Uhm." Grace licked her dry lips. "No. I'm fine. You have taken me by surprise is all." By bringing the most attractive guy she'd ever seen into her bedroom and dangling him in front of her like man-candy.

"I need you to get over it, like now. You said your name was Hobbs, right?" asked the annoying and scary fairy. "Grace Hobbs. And you're a witch." She looked around the room and its plethora of plants. The entire trailer was filled with greenery, some were for beauty, but most were for her potions and spellwork. "Wow. You really like plants."

"Forgive Zerina," said the good-looking man. "She has no

manners. I'm Tabor Standing Bear and this is my grandfather, Theobold. We're bear shifters from Arkansas."

"Technically, I live in Pawhuska, Oklahoma. But please call me Pops," said the old man. "Everyone does."

"I'm Liz," said Grace's familiar as she sauntered into the room. "Ta, Zerina."

"Ta, my ass, you puking gecko," muttered the fairy.

Tabor tipped his hat to Grace. "Nice to meet you." His deep voice, as smooth and rich as a late-night DJ's, made her whole body tingle right down to her toes. He had a light twang that served as a reminder he was Southern. Bear shifter, huh? That explained his height and muscular body. Grace tried not to stare as if Tabor were a roadside scenic view.

Liz crawled onto her shoulder, curling her tail around Grace's neck. She whispered, "That Tabor's a nice one. You could take 'em for a ride. Or better yet, he could take you for a ride. He's already wearing the hat."

Tabor's lips turned up in a sheepish grin. Shifter hearing. Ugh. Grace blushed to the roots of her hair. Dear Goddess, if she didn't get out of here, she was going to die of embarrassment.

Wait. No. This was her bedroom. It was everyone else who needed to leave. "Can I help you?"

"I hope so," said Patsy. "Because you're probably the only witch in the world who can."

CHAPTER 4

This is bullshit, Grace. Make 'em leave. Trust me when I say you don't want anything to do with those shifty bear shifters.

"Who's the old broad?" asked Patsy. She stared right at Dorcas. "A silver top and bootie shorts with those heels? Are you a retired stripper?"

I can wear what I want. I'm dead.

"Who the hell are you talking to?" asked Zerina. She squinted at the space next to Grace.

Patsy rolled her eyes. "I forget that not everyone can see ghosts."

"That shouldn't be possible. You're not a Hobbs." Bright hope dared to peek through the gray clouds of misery as Grace realized *someone else could see her ghost.* "No one else has ever been able to see Dorcas. Except me."

"And me," said Liz, who was tied to Grace through witch-familiar bonds. "Not that I ever want to."

Shut it you scaly bitch, or I'll hide your treats again.

Liz flickered her tongue in Dorcas's direction, but otherwise ignored the witch's threats.

"I have a lot more mojo than most vampires," said Patsy. "You got the queen part, right?"

"Oh, my sweet goddess on a gumdrop. I always look like I'm yelling at myself or berating the air around me," Grace told Patsy. Then she sighed. "And it gets even worse when Dorcas decides to go naked."

Hey! Body shaming a dead woman is not cool.

"Dorcas Hoar," muttered Pops. "Is that old crone is still haunting the Hobbs?"

Hey! Who you calling old crone?

Grace turned her stunned gaze to the old man. "You know about Dorcas?"

He nodded. "It's a tale that's been passed down through the years. The Curse of Deliverance Hobbs."

Fake news! yelled Dorcas. *Deliverance Hobbs was my curse. She stole my man. She was a horrible witch. A terrible person.*

Patsy's blonde eyebrows nearly hit her hairline. "Take it easy, Dorcas." She glanced at Pops. "Maybe you should share the story with the whole class."

"In the living room," added Grace, pointing toward her opened bedroom door. "Please."

Grace's gaze landed on Tabor, and she found him staring at her. His expression revealed nothing, but she could only imagine what he must be thinking. Probably something along the lines of "crazy" and "freak." Nothing she hadn't heard before. Now that she had the full attention of the bear shifter, she felt like a bug under a microscope. That was the total opposite of feeling sexy and desired.

Self-conscious, she tucked her hair behind her ear and led the way out of her bedroom into the small living room. There was only the one couch, which Zerina and Patsy claimed, so Grace brought in chairs from the kitchen for Tabor and Pops.

"Can I get you anything?" she asked. "Lemonade? Tea?"

"Sweet tea?" asked Pops.

"No, I'm afraid not."

Everyone stared at her.

"Where'd you say you were from, honey?" asked Patsy.

"California," admitted Grace.

"Ah. Well, around here, it ain't tea if it ain't sweet tea."

"It's a Southern thing," explained Zerina. "Trust me when I say you should embrace this concept."

Patsy nodded. "Now, you got any pie?"

Grace shook her head.

"See, the answer to that, always, is yes, followed by would you like apple or pecan?" Patsy smiled. "Any fruit is acceptable, of course."

"I don't like pie," said Grace.

Stunned silence met her admission.

"You must never utter those words again," said Patsy. "Do you understand?"

"Oh. Another Southern thing," said Grace.

"No, it's a bloody human being thing," said Zerina. "Who doesn't like pie?"

Patsy held up the tongs. "We need to have a long talk, Grace. But it'll have to wait until we discuss the undead bunnies situation." She clicked the tongs at Pops. "But the first thing I want to know is what's the deal with the Hobbs curse?"

Grace barely had time to process "undead bunnies" when Dorcas demanded, *Why don't you ask me? I'm standing right here. Floating. I'm floating right here.*

"Fine," said Patsy. She gestured to the ghost. "Tell us your version of events."

Dorcas crossed her arms, which brought attention to her sagging triceps acting as flap covers over her sagging boobs, wrinkled abs, and, oh goddess on a gondola, the flower tattoo around her navel.

Deliverance stole my boyfriend and married him. So, I cursed their cows. And their crops. And I may or may not have accidentally set their barn on fire.

"Wow," said Patsy. "You did all that over a dude?"

It was the 1600s. We didn't exactly have roaring social lives. You know what Deliverance did? Turned me into the magistrates for witchcraft, that's what. Those assholes drowned me! But Deliverance got hers, said Dorcas smugly. *I cast a spell that attached my spirit to her and to all of her firstborn female line.*

"Uh-huh." Patsy conveyed Dorcas's story to the others. Grace had heard it before. Many, many, many times. Dorcas wore her bitterness like expensive perfume. The vampire queen looked at the two bear shifters and Zerina. "Basically, she got pissed, messed shit up, then the Hobbs turned her in for her witchy ways, and they dunked her ass until she was dead. So, she cursed the Hobbs to have to put up with her shit till infinity."

That's not what I said, Dorcas huffed as she circled Grace's head.

Grace batted the ghost away. "Close enough."

"Our family stories are different," said Pops. "For one, the Hobbs didn't turn in Dorcas for witchcraft. But I can do better than that. With Deliverance's own words." He looked at Zerina. "Would you mind?"

"Yeah. Sure. Because I've always wanted to be a librarian." Zerina twirled her fingers.

A small well-worn leather-bound book appeared in the older bear shifter's hands. He thumbed through the yellowed pages until he found what he wanted. He read aloud:

"Dorcas Hoar has declared war on me because I dared to love Philip, and he to love me. She swore her vengeance upon us both when we married, and soon after we bespoke our vows, our farm was beset by the blackest of magic.

I desire only peace and harbor no ill will toward Dorcas, but her curses have roused suspicions. The magistrates arrested her, and she blames us for her predicament. And now we are to have a trial. Still more are accused of witchcraft every day. Dorcas has opened the door to madness. Salem has become a poisoned ground for witches."

Pops closed book. "It was Dorcas's use of magic to hurt Deliverance that got the attention of the humans in town and that led to the Salem witch trials. Once the local coven got wind of Dorcas's antics, they sought to bind her magic, but it was too late. Dorcas had been thrown into the nearest pond. It was a witch test concocted by humans. Supposedly, the innocent would sink like a stone and witches bobbed to the surface." Pops rolled his eyes. "It's a stupid test. Anyway. Dorcas drowned. Still, she managed one last trick: she bound herself to the Hobbs family. In her diary, Deliverance wrote that Dorcas Hoar swore she would drive the Hobbs women insane—and would spend her afterlife making sure no Hobbs woman would ever have love or marital happiness."

Grace looked at Dorcas, who immediately turned her gaze to the ceiling and said, *Deliverance always was a drama queen.*

Yeah, right. Grace's mother Nera had been the very last of the Hobbs line. She'd been determined not to have a child so that the curse ended with her death. Grace had been a complete surprise. Nera always believed Dorcas had somehow been responsible for a one-night-stand that begat Grace, but Dorcas denied she had anything to do with the witch getting knocked up. It didn't matter, though, did it?

Grace didn't know anything about her father, and since her mother was already half-insane from Dorcas' constant nagging, bitching, and fit-throwing, she wasn't exactly prime motherhood material. When Grace was nine-years-old, Nera put her in a California boarding school and moved to Europe. After Grace graduated high school, she received a registered letter from her mother with a check for $25,000. And never heard from Nera again.

Grace had been in her first year at the Sacramento School of Herbalism and Botanical Magic. Dorcas appeared in her dorm room, announced her mother had died on an alpine ski slope, and proceeded to destroy Grace's life. In fact, it took less than a month for Dorcas to get Grace expelled.

"So Dorcas is a bitch witch," said Zerina.

You think having the same gig for four-hundred-plus years is a picnic? I've endured centuries of dealing with ninnies like this one. Dorcas jabbed a thumb at Grace. *I hate people. They sucked when I was alive. And they suck even more now that I'm dead.* Dorcas' eyes bulged, and the air around her started to stir. Great. Dorcas was working herself up into a hissy fit. Dorcas rounded on Grace. *I know the Standing Bears. I was there when Deliver-Pain-in-My-Ass and Philip arrived to plant that stupid tree. You stay away from those bears, Grace Anne Hobbs!*

"Knock it off." Patsy lifted her hand and black sparkling ropes hissed toward Dorcas. They wrapped around her mouth, her shoulders, and her legs. She looked like she'd been taken hostage by an angry Kraken. Of course, no one else could see anything but the magic tendrils hovering in mid-air.

Grace's mouth dropped open. For the first time since Grace inherited the curse, Dorcas was quiet and still. She wanted to weep. Hell, she wanted to use the bathroom!

"Explain the tree thing to Grace," said Patsy.

"The Salem coven put their magic into a talisman called the *solic nigis cantatis* and gave it to Deliverance and Philip to go found another town. They ended up in Arkansas near the White River," said Pops. "The Hobbs made friends with the Osage Bear Clan shifters and formed a pact with us to always protect the magical tree."

"I'm the guardian," said Tabor. "There's not much left of

the old village. There's still the church and a few crumbling buildings in what used to be downtown. Now, Frank—the tree—is sick. Really sick. Its dying, and we don't know why or how to stop it."

"Only a few people know where the tree is," said Pops. "Keeping Frank's location secret is necessary to prevent misuse of its magical properties." He looked at Grace. "That's where you come in. We're hoping you can heal the tree."

Stunned, Grace stared at the bear shifters. "Me?"

"You're the only Hobbs left," added Tabor. "Since your ancestors used their spellwork to plant the tree, you might be the only witch who can save it."

"What does Grace get?" asked Zerina.

Tabor looked shocked that Zerina had asked such a question. Honestly, Grace was, too.

"Yeah, yeah," said Zerina. "Look at me. Giving a shit. What does Grace get for traipsing off to Hellhole, Arkansas with bear boy over there?"

"Well," said Pops. "There's a good chance that once we get Frank healed, you'll have the magic you need to break your curse."

Grace glanced at Dorcas and saw the woman's eyes go wide. She knew that Dorcas didn't want to leave the earthly plane. She liked haunting Grace and making her crazy, and it was probably better than the alternative for someone who'd lived her life and her death as selfishly as Dorcas.

Tabor looked at Grace, and she was utterly drawn in by those chocolate-y depths. "Will you come to Arkansas with me and heal Frank?"

"Yes," said Grace instantly. Her mouth hadn't even consulted with her brain. Damn those velvet brown eyes and tight jeans.

The magic spirals imprisoning Dorcas shattered into a

thousand glittering shards. Dorcas shrieked so loudly that the sound of it actually shook the trailer. Liz slithered off Grace and trotted under the table, yelling, "She's gonna blow, mate!"

Get rid of me, will you! Just try it, missy! Dorcas picked up Grace and tossed her into the air. Oh, sweet baby goddess! Dorcas had never laid hands on her before. Her eyes flew wide as she tried to brace for impact.

Two strong arms caught her. Tabor. His gaze filled with concern as he cuddled her against his broad, muscled chest. She could hear the strong beat of his heart beneath her ear. He smelled wonderful, like fresh-cut grass and sun-warmed soil. Those were two of her favorite scents. Botany magic was her life. She adored being arm deep in earth, soaking up the sunshine as eagerly as her plants.

And he smelled just like that. She inhaled deeply, trying not to be too obvious, and felt a wave of hot desire roll through her.

"She's never done that before," she said, working to control her shivers. "Thank you for catching me."

"My pleasure, Miss Hobbs."

His smile nearly melted her panties. She clung to him, staring, getting hotter by the minute. She had an insane urge to kiss him. *You smell like the outdoors. Like everything I love.* Grace resisted attacking his face with her lips, but she couldn't look away from the man.

"You gonna let her go?" asked Patsy. "Or do you plan to carry her all the way to Arkansas?" She looked up at Dorcas who'd blown her energy on assaulting Grace and now drifted at the top of the ceiling.

Liz's neck frill was sticking out like a cobra ready to strike as she switched her tail up toward the listless ghost. "Don't ever pull that shit again, you wally old hag."

It appeared Dorcas was too tired to even wield sarcasm,

but Grace saw the ghost's regretful expression. It was a rare moment when Dorcas was ashamed by her actions.

Tabor put Grace on her feet and steadied her until she felt strong enough to stand on her own. Liz scurried up Grace and curled around her neck, petting Grace's arm with her tail.

"I'm glad that's all settled." Zerina stood up. "Now, it's time to move along and go save trees and witches and shit."

"Okay. Zerina, you poof the bear shifters, and I'll get Grace and the lizard there. I assume Dorcas can find her own way." Patsy lifted the tongs and made a c'mere gesture at Grace.

Was this actually happening right now? Panic twisted through Grace. "What about clothes and spell books and Liz's toys—"

"I'll make sure your crappy trailer gets to Tabor's cabin," offered Zerina.

Before Grace had a chance to digest that bit of news, Patsy pulled Grace into her embrace. Liz clung harder to her witch's neck. "You might want to hold on," said the vampire.

Then everybody exploded.

CHAPTER 5

*W*hen Grace opened her eyes, she stood on the front porch of a log cabin. Patsy let her go and then patted her on the shoulder. "First time traveling by vampire?"

"Last time, too," said Grace.

Patsy laughed. "It takes some getting used to, but it's not so bad."

"Says you." Liz trembled on Grace's shoulder. "Bugger all. Let's never do that again."

Grace's stomach felt queasy. If she could help it, she was never using vampire travel again. She turned and looked at the gloomy, tangled woods beyond a small clearing. Her nausea subsided. The night sky was studded with stars and a crescent moon. It smelled like earth and pine and wood smoke. She instantly felt at home.

How odd. It wasn't like her little trailer was uncomfortable, but there was something special about Tabor's space. She shouldn't be surprised that a bear shifter lived in the woods. She didn't know much about Arkansas, but its beauty soothed her soul. She could feel the peace of the surrounding nature right down to her bones.

I've seen better. Dorcas floated next to her. When she got sullen, she often presented herself as a Puritan with a white bonnet and a simple black dress. But she still wore the clear plastic high heels that had accompanied her previous outfit. *How long are we supposed to be at this dump?*

Grace didn't answer. She didn't want to inspire another Dorcas temper tantrum by reminding the ghost they were here to heal a magical tree so Grace could break the family curse.

Next to her, the air began to fill with gold sparkles. Tabor and Pops appeared, and between them was Zerina holding each of their arms. Tabor looked like he never wanted to burst into nothingness ever again. Tabor took off his hat, and Grace saw his brown hair, which he wore long enough to curl around his ears. The hatband had pressed a circle around his head, which she thought was adorable. He ran a hand through his thick locks.

"I appreciate the...er, ride," said Grace. "Thanks."

"Nothing like a vampire taxi service," said Patsy.

What the holy fuck tits are those things? screamed Dorcas.

"Get inside," yelled Pops as the little white and scabby things tumbled around both corners of the cabin and scrambled toward them. The stench wafting from the creatures nearly curled Grace's nose hairs. "Hurry!"

Tabor opened the door and everyone piled inside.

Unfortunately, some of the creatures hopped in right behind them. Tabor managed to shut the door before more of the hellions could get inside.

Pops squawked and ran into the kitchen.

"What's happening?" asked Grace. Liz clung so hard to her shoulders the familiar's little claws embedded into her skin.

"We have a zombie rabbit issue," said Zerina, kicking away decrepit rabbits like she was auditioning for the Rockettes. "We think it's because of the tree."

Holy shitballs! We have a breach! We have a breach! Dorcas pointed at a rogue bunny doing a one-legged hop toward Grace.

Tabor had procured a baseball bat and bashed the roadkill before it got within ankle-biting distance. Patsy was smacking others away with her tongs, using obscenities Grace hadn't ever heard before. Dorcas was zipping back and forth in sheer panic trying to point out the obvious.

"I thought you could control zombies, Patsy," said Zerina.

"Not these little fuckers. I've already tried ten ways to Sunday to command them. They ain't listening." Patsy glared at Zerina. "Why aren't you using your mighty fairy magic to do something about this shit?"

"Because my fairy magic doesn't work on zombies," said Zerina. "Duh." She swung around to glare at Grace. "What about you? Can't you whip up a spell or something?"

"I can try," said Grace. Her magic was attached to nature and to healing what was alive—and these rabbits were animated, but obviously deceased. Still, she had to give it a shot. She inhaled deeply, gathered her magic, and released it toward the hopping dead as she shouted, *"Ad mortem!"*

Nothing happened. The bunnies ignored the spell as easily as Dorcas ignored Grace's bathroom privacy.

"How do we get rid of this army of evil furriness?" asked Pops as he returned to the living room holding a frying pan. He jumped onto the couch and waved it. His eyes were wide as saucers as he surveyed the madness around them.

"All we got left is the Bunny Fu-Fu method!" shouted Patsy.

Grace reached for the nearest thing she could find—a *Cosmopolitan* magazine. She twisted it into a thick roll and batted at the undead bunnies trying to attack her feet. Liz scurried off Grace's shoulders and took off under the couch.

A nanosecond later, Liz scrambled out, followed by a teeth-gnashing bunny with one dangling eye. Grace swept the bunny away with a flick of the magazine. Liz scurried away to parts unknown—and hopefully, dead-bunny-free.

"Not the *Cosmo*," complained Pops. "I haven't taken the *Are You A Sexy Beast?* quiz yet."

"Priorities, old man," said Zerina. "Also, no. You are not a sexy beast. What's wrong with you?"

"These little fuckers are fast," said Patsy. "Don't they know they're dead? Where's all the shambling, and the shuffling, and falling off of decomposing parts to slow them down?" A rotted rabbit growled at her, flashing fangs. She hissed and bashed its head with the tongs then she kicked it across the room. It left a greenish red smear along the hardwood floors. "Yuck! Now I have rabbit guts on my feet."

"That's it," declared Pops. "We're going to have to burn the whole house down."

~

From his hiding spot in the tree line, Lucas stared at the sea of undead bunnies attacking the log cabin. It seemed an ineffective way to rid the area of the bear shifter guardian, if that was, indeed, the purpose of the rabbits. Lucas couldn't be sure why the bunny army had swarmed the area. Nothing about the encroaching horde appeared organized and he figured the dead-rabbit attack was a symptom of the true cause.

The *Franklinia Magica* was dying.

Lucas lifted his hands and whispered, "*Mortuus est ergo iterum mori.*"

It only took a moment for his necromancer magic to take hold of the undead vermin. Their tiny corpses went inert.

He couldn't do much about the bunnies that had gotten into the house, but for the ones outside—he whispered another spell, and the ground underneath the rabbits went soft as pudding. They sank deeply into the earth and within less than a minute, every tiny dead thing was nestled under the soil, never to rise again.

Lucas debated about making his presence known to those who were in the cabin. Yeah, sure. He could knock on the door and when they opened it to see an immortal necromancer standing on their porch, he could announce, "Hi! I'm from the underworld and by the way, so is the thing that's killing your tree. Sorry about that!"

No, it was better if he dealt with the problem himself.

Decision made, Lucas slipped back through the forest and headed back to the church.

~

The bunny horde dropped to the floor, inanimate, and finally dead. Dead-dead, not undead-dead. One minute everybody was battling their way through mangled, feral furballs and the next, they were standing in the middle of the room, huffing, sweating, and holding blood-soaked weapons.

"I'm not cleaning this up," Zerina said, looking around at the littered bodies. "I'm going home to burn my clothes. I'll get your trailer here tomorrow, Grace." The fairy wiggled her finger at the witch. "You owe me."

"I'm going with you," said Pops. He dropped the frying pan onto the floor and grabbed Zerina's arm. "I want to visit the senior citizen nudist colony in Broken Heart."

"Just kill me," muttered Zerina. Gold sparkled and the two disappeared.

Patsy looked at her tongs, her splattered feet, and then at the carnage. "Yeah. I'm outta here, too. Night, kids." She, too, left in a shower of gold magic.

Only Liz, Grace, and Tabor remained.

We should leave, too, said Dorcas. *Who cares about that stupid tree?*

Oh, yeah. And her nemesis.

"I care, Dorcas." Grace turned to Tabor. "I'm worried about the tree. If it sent the zombie rabbits as a signal for help, then this de-animation might mean it's getting weaker."

"Maybe. Pops said the tree might've have something to do with this mess," said Tabor. "But the tree has never enacted magic on its own. Look, it's too late to go out to the church and check on Frank today. We'll have to save it for the morning." He looked around. "I better get the lawn garbage bags."

"No need," said Grace. She lifted her hands and muttered one of many cleaning spells she'd memorized. She'd learned more than a dozen of them, and they came in handy given the messes so often made by Dorcas.

The zombie bunnies disappeared. And then all the gore they left behind disappeared, too. "What do you want to do about the frying pan? I mean, I could clean it, but…"

"Uh, no. I'll get a new one."

Grace clapped her hands and the pan disappeared, too.

"Wow," said Tabor. "Thanks. You're amazing."

Grace glowed under the small praise. Then she heard a series of rattles and crashes. She followed the sounds into the kitchen and found an overturned table and piles of broken dishes and mangled food items.

Dorcas hovered above the mess, arms crossed, looking supremely satisfied.

"Breakfast for dinner," explained Tabor as he kneeled to

pick up pieces of a shattered bowl. "Pops and I never got around to eating."

"Let me," said Grace softly. "I'm afraid Dorcas is the one who ruined your dinner."

Tabor smiled. "No. The zombie bunnies did that."

Grace muttered another cleaning spell. The dishes and food disappeared and the table righted itself.

"That's a handy little gift you have there," said Tabor. "I appreciate it."

"No problem." Grace felt warmed to her toes by the bear shifter's smile. "Do you have a blanket I can use?" She nodded toward the couch.

"Nonsense. You and your lizard—"

"I have a name," the familiar said.

"Liz," Grace supplied.

Tabor nodded. "You and Liz," he acknowledged the frill-neck familiar. "You two take my bed, and I'll take the couch."

"Thank you." Grace gazed at Tabor, and damn, her heart went pitty-pitty-pat. At least until Dorcas floated down in front of her and gave her the stink eye.

You keep making goo-goo eyes at that bear shifter, and I'll sing 99 Bottles of Beer *all night long. And I'll destroy more than his dinner, too.*

Grace gave Dorcas the win. She didn't have a choice. But if Pops had been right about the ancient tree—then Grace might actually be free of the old hag very, very soon.

And that was worth everything.

~

"Iloooooost my girl, my truck, and my ol' coooooon dog," lamented a singer with a gruff voice.

Tabor opened one eye, reached down and shut off his

radio alarm. The digital screen glowed 5:00 a.m., and it was still dark outside. He was suffering from a fairy transport hangover. For whatever reason, every time he moved through space and time with Zerina, it just about killed him.

Why the hell did he set his alarm? Flat on his stomach, sprawled on the couch, the television's remote control puncturing what was probably his liver, it took him a minute to figure out why the hell he was on his couch and not sprawled in his bear-sized bed.

Oh, yeah. Grace Hobbs.

Grace was a different kind of witch, and not just because of the curse. She seemed to lack the cocky confidence exhibited by most witches. In a way, Tabor found her quirky, seemingly shy, nature endearing. Besides, Grace smelled like deep, rich, sweet honey. The kind you get right out of the hive. He wasn't going to read too much into that because bears loved honey, and he was no exception. He wasn't going to think about the family stories about the mate-honey smell. Pops and Grandma Beth claimed they'd both caught the scent. And his parents did, too.

He smiled as he thought about Grace's sexy curves, her imp-like nose, turned up the tiniest bit on the end, and the largest, greenest eyes he'd ever seen. Even her purple-gold hair suited her, and he'd wanted to run his fingers through the silky strands and—

Goddess, help me. I'm like a lovesick teenager.

Tabor tried to remind himself that Grace had only agreed to investigate the tree problem because Zerina had told her its magic might be enough to lift her curse. He couldn't hear or see the ghostly witch that haunted her, but if Grace's reactions were any indication, Dorcas Hoar made a hornet look cuddly.

Mate. Mate. Mate. She's your mate. Admit it. Then get on with the courting.

That voice sounded a lot like his mother's. Ugh. He pulled the remote out from underneath him and tossed it on the coffee table. Just as he closed his eyes, the radio went off again. He uncurled an arm and attempted to smack the annoying device. His balance shifted, and he rolled off the couch. The back of his head thwacked the clock, pushing several buttons. The alarm and the radio blared to life, intensifying the cracked-skull ache creeping across his scalp. He yanked the cord out of the wall. This morning he would need coffee with his coffee.

Knock, knock, knock.

Someone banging on his door at this hour could not have good news. He scrambled up and banged his knee on the heavy oak wood coffee table. After ten seconds of hopping and cursing, he limped to the door of his cabin and opened it.

"This better be—" Tabor blinked. Witchling Protectress Helen Montrose stood on the porch. On either side of her were two little girls who clung to her hands as if she were the only buoy in a raging sea.

"Hi, Tabor," said Helen. "We need your help."

CHAPTER 6

*T*abor stepped aside and allowed the children and Helen into the cabin. He ushered them into the front area, removing the blanket from the leather couch to make room for the girls. Twins. They looked they were about five years old. They stared up at him, silent, their big blue eyes wide with exhaustion and terror.

"I have the comfiest couch in the whole state of Arkansas," he said. "You want to try it out?"

They looked at each other, and the sweetheart on the left said, "Yes, sir."

"I'm Tabor," he said gently. "I don't mind at all if you want to use my name."

"I'm Eden," said the talkative girl. She glanced at her sister and tilted her head in Tabor's direction.

"I'm Erin." Erin had a dimple on the right side of her mouth—the only feature she didn't share with her sister.

"Hi Erin and Eden. Hey, do y'all like *Frozen*?"

He kept an array of animated movies on hand because he didn't have cable or satellite. Getting those kind of services in the middle of nowhere was nigh on impossible and for another, he wasn't keen on strangers wandering around his land. Despite the fact the town had been gone for more than two centuries and Frank wasn't well known even to parakind, he couldn't risk the wrong kind of people finding out about the ancient magic Frank held.

Tabor and has family had been a stop in the underground for—well, ever since he could remember. His grandparents and his parents had hosted supernatural beings who needed to escape from their abusers and potential killers. As the Arkansas Witchling Protectress, Helen was in charge of investigating witchling abuse and neglect claims in the state. The job was not one for the faint of heart, and Tabor knew she'd charge hell with a bucket of ice water if it meant saving a child. However, when the endangered witchlings in question could not be removed through proper channels and Helen felt they were in imminent danger then she relied on other means to secure their safety.

By bringing the girls to him, and given the expression on her face and the fatigue making her shoulders slump, Tabor knew she was putting the girls into what equaled parakind's unofficial witness protection program.

He aimed the remote at the big-screen television, turned it on, and then slid the disc into the player. "You girls want something drink? Are you hungry?"

Once again the sisters looked at each other, and Erin said, "No, thank you, sir."

They settled onto the couch and stared joylessly at the movie. *Poor babies,* he thought. *Somebody's sucked the happiness right outta them.*

He led Helen beyond the living area to the kitchen. He leaned against the counter and asked, "Are you okay?"

"We got away clean."

"Who are they, Helen?"

"The twin daughters of a very powerful warlock. I

45

rescued them in Little Rock. Yours was the first place I thought of, Tabor. I need you to protect the girls while I make arrangements for them to disappear."

"What happened to them?" he asked softly.

"Their asshole father is channeling their power to supplement his own. Without training, they don't know how to protect themselves. The power drain is affecting their health and their magical abilities." Helen's eyes gleamed with fury. "Their human mother died in childbirth. Dad's a well-connected, wealthy warlock."

"Not that stealing their magic isn't horrible enough, but..." Tabor trailed off and let Helen interpret what he was asking.

"If you're wondering about other types of abuse, the answer is no." She shook her head. "The girls told me that he never hit them. Or hugged them, for that matter. I'm not sure he even spoke to them outside of the times he siphoned their magical abilities. But even so, living in a loveless, cold home with an uncaring father—I don't imagine that was very good for their emotional and mental wellbeing. They're only five years old, Tabor. If it wasn't for their new nanny reporting the situation to me...I don't know what would've happened to them."

Tabor rubbed his jaw. "You said he was a warlock, huh? Have you reported anything to the Arkansas Witch Council?"

"After I've gotten the girls away, I'll report Asshole Dad for magical larceny. He's probably up to his eyeballs in all kinds of black arts, personal gain spells, and abuse of Mother Earth." She sighed. "I can't risk Eden and Erin's safety right now. Unfortunately, their father has connections up the wazoo." She rubbed her face, her weariness evident. "I fear members of the council might owe him favors."

Tabor felt a tug on his blue sweats. He looked down at the little girl standing next to him. He knew by the dimple that dotted the right corner of her lips that this was Erin. "Are you really a bear?" she asked in a tiny, sweet voice.

Tabor smiled. "Sometimes." He squatted down so he was eye-level. "I can shift into a bear."

She seemed pleased by his admission. "Good."

"She thinks you can protect us from our father," intoned Eden. Tabor switched his gaze to the other girl who now stood near the couch. Her expression was serious and her eyes so devoid of emotion that his chest felt hollow.

"He's mean," said the urchin clinging to him. She leaned forward and whispered, "He hurts us."

Tabor felt his heart constrict in his chest. "It's okay, honey," he said. "He won't hurt you ever again." He stroked her hair. "Why don't you go watch TV with your sister?"

She nodded and rejoined Eden. The twins scooted onto the couch. He watched Eden put her arm around her sister and bring her in close—a protective gesture. What kind of cold-hearted bastard thought of his children as magical batteries? He wanted to go shifter and rip the guy to shreds.

Tabor drew Helen further into the kitchen. "I have a...guest. A witch."

Helen's eyebrows rose and her expression said: *Booty call? Really?* "I wouldn't ask if it wasn't urgent, Tabor."

"Grace isn't here for...uh, me. She's doing some magical healing. For nature. Around the cabin." Helen didn't know about Frank. In fact, almost no one knew about the magical tree, and for good reason. If warlocks existed that would siphon magic from little girls, he could only imagine what the morally corrupt would do if presented with a tree that held ancient magic from a thirteen-witch coven. Most folks thought he lived out in the boonies because he liked being a hermit. Not true. But like his parents and grandparents and the Standing Bears before them, he felt a powerful duty to protect the *Franklinia Magica*.

47

"Tabor?"

"Yeah." He ran his fingers through his hair. He needed caffeine to stimulate his brain cells. Taking care of two adorable little girls had not been on the menu this week. He only had the one bedroom upstairs, and Grace was already snug in his bed. Where the heck was he going to put witch-lings? "I'm not saying no," he said carefully. "How long do you need?"

"Two, maybe three days to get them new identities and passage through the underground."

"Okay," Tabor said, "I'll make it work."

~

*G*race stood on the last step of the back staircase and shamelessly listened to the hushed conversation between Tabor and the witch named Helen. When she'd gone to bed, she'd enjoyed wrapping herself up in covers that smelled like the bear shifter. Even when she'd heard the voices downstairs, she'd been reluctant to leave the snug Tabor-scented cocoon.

Dorcas floated next to her, dressed in booty shorts and a tank top, her gray locks pulled into a Madonna-esque ponytail.

Saves orphans and melts the hearts of single witches every-where. Dorcas rolled her eyes. *That one has a total god complex.*

"Knock it off." Grace glared at Dorcas. She remembered too well what it had been like in boarding school. For all intents and purposes, she was an orphan. She'd never gone home on the holidays like the other students. Even so, it hadn't been an unpleasant childhood—and was better than what she would've gotten from her mother—but it was defi-nitely not the same as growing up with a loving family. Witches and warlocks would come and go—nurses, teachers, headmistresses, cooks, coaches, and everyone else. No one stayed forever. The witches and warlocks who saw her off into her adult life were not the same ones who'd taken her in at the age of nine.

Your bear in furry armor is leaving with his lady friend.

"Stay here," said Grace. "Please, Dorcas. Those little girls must be scared out of their wits."

Dorcas frowned then she shrugged. *Fine. I'll stay here.*

After Tabor had walked Helen out the front door, Grace left the stairs and went through the kitchen. She ventured into the living room and rounded the couch, staying about a foot away.

"Hello," she said to the twins. "My name is Grace Hobbs. But you can call me Grace, if you like."

"Hi. I'm Eden. This is Erin." The young girl studied her. Eden's hair was a shade darker blonde than her sister's. And Erin had an adorable dimple on the right side of her mouth.

"You're pretty," they said together. "We like your hair."

"Thank you," said Grace, inordinately pleased with the compliment. When a witch had a Dorcas hanging over her shoulder pummeling her self-esteem every day, even the prettiest of witches could get a complex. "You and your sister are very pretty, too."

"Thank you, Grace." Once again, the girls spoke in one voice.

She stepped a little closer. She wanted to hug the bad right out of them, but forcing her affection would probably be more detrimental than good for the twins. She imagined they had serious trust issues when it came to adults.

"Are you the bear shifter's wife?" asked Erin.

"Um, no. I'm his—." What was she exactly? They hadn't known each other long enough to be friends. "His colleague," she finally said. It felt inadequate, but it would have to do.

Both the girls looked at her, their expressions this side of suspicious.

"Is a colleague like a boyfriend?" asked Eden.

Before she could respond to that question, Tabor re-entered the house. He looked surprised to see Grace standing in front of the girls, but he recovered quickly. "Grace. I see you've met our new guests."

Tabor was barefoot. His hair was messed up from sleep. He wore blue sweat pants, and that was it. His broad, muscled chest was the size of Arkansas. Six-pack? Sweet baby goddess. Try twelve-pack. His chest and stomach were lightly furred, and the brown curls arrowed down into the sweats. She was dying to have a peek inside.

"She likes your boobs," said Erin matter-of-factly.

Grace felt her face go hot.

Tabor grinned. "Oh, yeah? How do you know?"

"Because she keeps staring at them," pointed out Eden. "Do you like her boobs?"

"I haven't seen her boobs," said Tabor. He flinched as the words exited his mouth.

Grace flinched too. This conversation was verging on humiliating.

Erin waved at her. "Fair's fair. You should let him see yours."

Dorcas appeared next to her guffawing so hard she bent over at the waist and gasped for air. Why did she insist on going through actions like she was still a human?

Yeah, Grace, show Mr. Bear your boobies.

Eden and Erin stared to the left of Grace, right where Dorcas was laughing her ass off.

"Hello," they said together. "Who are you?"

Dorcas was shocked into silence.

So was Grace. It took her second of gathering her wits before she could ask, "You can see the lady?"

"She's not alive," said Erin.

"That's right," said Grace. "She's a ghost."

Eden stared at Dorcas. "Why are you naked?"

Grace looked at the spirit. Yep. The witch was buck-assed naked.

What the hell is going on? Dorcas looked astonished. *I didn't take off my clothes, I swear.*

"Why do your boobs hang down that far?" asked Erin.

"Your skin is wrinkly like an elephant's," said Eden.

The twins took turns asking rapid-fire questions and making blunt comments. Grace's wide smile turned into peals of unstoppable laughter.

"Why does your face look like it's sliding off?"

"Your hair looks funny. Didn't you brush it today?"

"What's that patch of hair between your legs?"

Grace laughed so hard she snorted. "Oh, Goddess." She grabbed her sides. "That hurts."

"Is it a bunch of spiders?"

"It looks like a bunch of *squished* spiders."

Grace choked on her spit.

Apparently, Dorcas was so stupefied at first that she forgot she was a ghost. Then she snapped out of it, gave Grace the finger, and popped out of the room. She didn't even bother with a parting sarcastic jibe.

Grace wiped her eyes. "I haven't laughed like that since...well...I can't remember."

"You should laugh more often," said Tabor. "It's a beautiful sound."

Tabor crossed the room to stand next to her. Instantly, the fresh-cut grass and fresh-dirt smell wafted around her. Something about this man made her want to throw herself into his arms and yell, "Take me!"

She met his gaze, and her pulse jumped. Something had changed. She wasn't quite sure what, but the look Tabor was giving her bordered on lascivious. Her heart started to pound. The way he looked at her made her belly flutter. She had this feeling he wanted to embrace her. Maybe even kiss her. *Yes, please.*

Tabor turned toward the twins and grinned. "So how naked was poor ol' Dorcas?"

"Very naked," said Eden and Erin together, giggling.

Tabor's expression turned mock serious. "I'm sorry you had to see that."

"I am, too," said Grace, trying to mimic Tabor's all-business countenance.

Tabor squatted down so he was eye level with the twins. "You girls must be exhausted. I've got a huge bed upstairs. It's like sleeping on a cloud. How does that sound?" He looked up at Grace. "I can make a pallet on the floor and you can take the couch."

Eden and Erin shared a look and then Eden reluctantly nodded. Both girls had a forlorn expression edged with fear. Grace figured they didn't want to crawl into a strange bed in a strange house. She knew from experience how awful it was to be utterly alone with people you didn't know—dropped off there by a person who no longer wanted you. In their case, they were escaping from the person who was supposed to love them. Only five-years-old and they'd already experienced too much suffering.

"Well, who wants to sleep in a plain ol' bed?" asked Grace. "We should make a couch and blanket fort and sleep inside it."

The girls' eyes widened.

"You can do that?" asked Erin. Her voice was pure wonder.

"Won't it mess up the living room?" Eden bit her lower lip, obviously concerned.

"Yep," said Tabor, jumping on board with the idea. "But

living rooms can't be tidy all the time. So, I'm obligated to officially mess it up. You want to help?"

The girls clapped, excited. Grace's heart turned over in her chest. *I'll protect you,* she promised them. She watched Tabor tossed off pillows and cushions. He laughed when the twins joined in. The deep rumble sounded like happy thunder. He met her eyes, just for a second, and her insides melted into a puddle. *And so will he,* Grace thought. *He'll protect you two no matter what.*

"You can't make a fort without me," Liz said as she waddled into the living room. She went to the girls. "Everyone knows you need a lizard to make any kind of fort."

"I didn't know that," said Erin.

Liz winked. "Well, you do now, girls."

The sisters knelt in front of Grace's familiar and stroked her head and back. Liz closed her eyes and emitted a low trill of satisfaction.

"Under the chin a bit, please."

Eden complied.

Liz opened her eyes and stared at the black Mary Janes. She licked all four them, no doubt marking the patent leather shoes for later snackage.

"Don't you even think about it, Liz. There's nobody in a thousand miles to fix you if you make yourself sick again.

"I can't help it," said Liz. "Mary Janes are my favorite."

CHAPTER 7

*G*race awoke to the sound of hushed voices. After making the couch fort with its blanket ceiling, they'd all crawled under it. Grace told the girls stories until they fell asleep.

She smiled. Neither Tabor nor Liz had lasted through the first bedtime tale, and their competing snores made the girls giggle. Hmm. Somehow, she'd ended up with a girl on either side of her, both hugging her as they slept. Tabor had given them two of his shirts for sleepwear. They were swallowed up by the material, which covered their feet and dragged across the floor. She couldn't help herself. She hugged them lightly. Sweet Goddess. She felt the warm fuzzies hardcore. How could anyone hurt them? How could a father trade the love of his daughters for their powers? *Asshole.*

"G'day," said Liz as she poked her head underneath the blanket. "It's after ten a.m., Grace. You getting up?"

"Yes," whispered Grace. She slowly extracted herself from the tiny arms and legs and scooted toward her familiar. The girls rolled toward each other and lay on the pillow, shoulder-to-shoulder, still sleeping, thank the Goddess. Liz backed up as Grace crawled out.

Huh. Someone was noticeably absent. It was the first day ever that Grace had awakened without Dorcas hovering above her, singing obnoxiously or reciting ribald limericks. She was surprised to realize she was concerned. *When did I start caring about that crazy witch?*

"Have you seen Dorcas?" she asked her familiar.

Liz flicked out her tongue. "That piker is clinging to the bedroom ceiling dressed in her Puritan best. Hasn't said bugger all for hours." Liz stood up on her hind legs. "Which is all right by me. First time I've been able to hear myself think in ages." She lifted her front leg and pointed at an opened suitcase. "That appeared here a few minutes ago. I opened it, but Zerina didn't put my treats inside."

Grace bent down and looked at the contents. Clothes, sneakers, and a wooden box inscribed with spells related to the seeds inside.

"Grace?" Tabor's voice called to her from the kitchen. "Do you have a moment?"

Grace got to her feet. Liz crawled up her side and settled in her usual place around Grace's neck. Grace walked into the kitchen. Tabor, dressed in a short-sleeved blue shirt with pearl snap buttons, a belt with a huge silver buckle, tight-assed jeans, and cowboy boots, sat at the island across from a curvy brunette who looked to be in her fifties. She had the same eyes as Tabor and the same color of hair. Grace guessed she was looking at Tabor's mother.

"Good morning, ma'am," said Grace. She smiled shyly at the bear shifter. "Hi, Tabor."

Tabor returned the smile. She saw his nose wiggle as if he were sniffing something in the air. She found herself mirroring the action. Yep. The warm earth fragrance wrapped around her. She found both hot-cocoa-soft-blanket comfort and holy-hot-pants-sexy times in that wonderful scent. *It's him,* she admitted. Tabor smelled like the outdoors and felt like home.

"Mom, this is Grace Hobbs and her familiar, Liz."

"Your trailer is here, sweetie," said Tabor's mom. She pointed out the kitchen window. "Zerina popped it in about ten minutes ago. Damn near took out a squirrel gathering nuts."

Grace looked out the window, wincing at the big dent in the blue aluminum siding near the screened door, before turning her attention back to the woman. "Please call me Grace."

"I'm Rhoda." Her sweet smile shifted into a wide grin. "So, Grace. How does it feel to be a bear shifter's mate?"

~

*T*abor felt embarrassed heat crawl up the back of his neck and start cooking his face. *I should've never told her about the honey jitters.* He was a fucking full-grown bear, yet his mom could still make him feel like a cub. It didn't help that Grace had taken the mating news as though she'd been told she was going to die of a terminal disease. Liz, however, looked absolutely delighted. Great. He'd impressed the lizard, but not her witch.

"Mom," he groaned.

"What?" she asked unabashedly. "How was I supposed to know you hadn't told her yet?" She winked at Grace. "I'm trying to help you, son."

Grace looked deathly pale and started to sway. Tabor cursed under his breath as he got up and guided Grace to the seat he'd just occupied. He poured her a glass of cold water from the filtered pitcher he kept in the fridge and put it in her hands. "Drink, sweetheart," he coaxed.

"It's not a death sentence, you know," said Rhoda. "I mean, I know the boy's ugly as sin, but he's handy to have around."

"Ugly?" asked Grace vaguely. She looked up at him, her eyes as round as saucers. "Who is she talking about?"

"Me."

She sipped the water and turned her gaze to Rhoda. "Do you have a vision problem?"

Rhoda pounded the butcher block and hooted. "I like you, Grace." She pointed at her. "You're a keeper. The Standing Bear honey jitters are never wrong." She tapped the side of her nose. "That's the way it works with our family."

Liz slithered off Grace's neck and stood up, using her clawed front feet to pat the witch's cheeks. "Grace? You all right?"

"I'm fine. I'm good." She stared at Tabor. "I can't...we can't...you know. I'd ruin your life. I can't foist my curse onto you." She paled even more. "I can't have kids, either. Dorcas will transfer to my firstborn daughter."

"I know all about the Hobbs' curse. And I agree with my father-in-law. Once you restore Frank, you'll be able to remove Dorcas," said Rhoda confidently. "You won't have worry about curses and spirits and what-not." She smiled at Grace. "Don't be so surprised, honey. The Standing Bear family has been protecting Frank for a long time. We are all very familiar with its history. Besides, I know my boy. And he is completely done in when it comes to you."

Tabor stroked Grace's back and hated that she was trembling. "Mom, stop it. You're overwhelming Grace." On the up side, the beautiful witch hadn't exactly said no to being his mate—and she'd immediately started thinking about children.

"What are the honey jitters?" asked Grace.

"When a Standing Bear finds his or her mate," Rhoda stared off in the distance as if captured by a sweet memory, "we're overwhelmed by this intense smell of honey. You can't get enough, ever. Every time I'm around my mate, it's as if we're still on our honeymoon. I want to eat him up from head to toe."

"TMI, Mom." But for the first time he understood exactly what his parents and grandparents had been talking about since he was old enough to hear the honey jitters stories. He wanted Grace Hobbs heart and soul, and he wasn't sure he could live without her. The intensity of those feelings damned near terrified him.

Grace frowned. "I don't have honey jitters. I mean...I don't smell any honey. But...Tabor," she inhaled deeply, turning her nose in his direction, "you smell like fresh-cut grass and sun-warmed soil. Like the smell of my greenhouse in the morning."

Tabor felt himself preen at her description. He didn't know how to feel about that. It wasn't like he expected his mate to enter his life yesterday. He'd actually gotten to the point where he thought he wouldn't mate. Some shifters never did. Even some Standing Bears had been bachelors their whole lives.

Grace seemed to enjoy his light back rub, so he kept doing it. She unconsciously leaned into it, and he moved his hands from her back to her shoulders. As he worked out the knotted muscles around her neck, she sighed with pleasure. That little noise went straight to his groin and stirred his blood. Crap. The last thing he needed right now was a hard-on. Especially with his mother in the room.

"How about we table the whole mating discussion?" he asked. "Grace has a tree to heal."

"Right," said Grace. "What he said."

"Mom's here to watch the twins. They'll be in good hands while I take you to Frank."

"I'll stay here, too," said Liz.

Grace nodded. "Okay. I'll get dressed." He saw Grace give her familiar the stink eye. "Don't eat anything I wouldn't."

The lizard's expression was all innocence. The fact that Liz could even have an expression blew Tabor's mind. Familiars talked and emoted like humans, but they didn't have dual natures like shifters. They had the kind of unbreakable and loving bond with their witches that Tabor had only seen between mates.

Tabor watched Grace slide off the stool and head toward the back staircase. Her gait was unsteady. As soon as she was out of earshot, Tabor said, "You about scared her to death." He stared daggers at his mother. "Why did you tell her she was my mate? You don't know that. Not for sure."

"The hell I don't. I know you Tabor Gareth Standing Bear. You'd hem and haw and overthink the whole situation, and by the time you figured out what to do, she'd be gone." Rhoda met his gaze, unashamed by her bold matchmaking. "Finding your mate has nothing to do with pros and cons lists and charts and Goddess knows what else your OCD mind comes up with. It's simple, son. When you find the one, you mate with her."

"Well, I think she has something to say about it," said Tabor drolly.

Rhoda waved as though she was flicking away his doubts. "I recognize the honey jitters, and believe me when I say that witch has 'em bad for you."

⁓

When Grace entered Tabor's bedroom, she saw Dorcas floating horizontally, her nose an inch away from the ceiling. She stared at the big planks that created the roof of the cabin. She was still dressed Puritan all the way, even with the buckle shoes and her hair neatly tucked into her plain white bonnet.

"Dorcas?"

The ghost slowly rolled until she faced the floor. Grace stepped underneath the sullen spirit so she could make eye contact. "Are you all right?"

What do you care? I'm a curse. A crazy witch. A ghost that should be sliced off you like an unwanted wart.

Grace couldn't deny any of those comments, but she wasn't entirely heartless. "Aren't you tired of being transferred person to person with no choice about whom you're with or where you can go?"

Well, that's my own fault, isn't it? I was so mad at Deliverance and Philip. I just wanted to cause them pain. Especially Deliverance. Dorcas sighed. *She was my best friend, you know. And she knew that Philip had come courting. But he took one look at her, and that was it.* Dorcas pressed her hands against her face. *When the spell took hold after I died, I aged into this...this old-hag body. No matter what I try to change about this form, I can't change that.* She looked at Grace. *That's what happens when you use magic to harm others, when you use it for selfish reasons. Threefold, it comes back to you.*

This was the first time Dorcas and Grace had had a real conversation. Most of their interactions involved yelling and throwing things. It had never occurred to Grace that Dorcas might feel scared or lonely. She wondered if any of her ancestors had cared about Dorcas. Was it even possible to have empathy for a contentious asshat? Or had Dorcas' own fear and bitterness crafted her into a ghost who'd rather be hated than rejected?

I don't know what will happen to me if you break the curse. I'm terrified about what's on the other side. She crossed her arms and sniffed. *And you know what? Those kids got to me. And they made fun of my hoo-ha. It's not like we had wax or lasers to tame the wilds down there back in the day.*

Grace swallowed a laugh because Dorcas sounded really upset. She cautiously wondered if this was a Dorcas trick. She'd fall for this sympathetic version and then get water dumped on her or tormented with atrocious singing until she wanted to rip off her own ears.

Four hundred years gave a witch-ghost a long time to learn how to do certain things. While Dorcas could change clothes and hairstyles easily, she'd never been able to re-craft her body. When she went on her naked sprees, she did it full-on-old-lady-style.

How did they make my clothes disappear? I mean, they're just witchlings. And they're not Hobbs relatives, either. They shouldn't be able to see me.

"That is strange." Grace frowned. It would be just like Dorcas to get naked and toss the blame at children. On the other hand, the woman seemed genuinely perplexed about the whole incident. "You're saying the twins undressed you?"

Well, I didn't do it.

"Why would they?"

How am I supposed to know? Maybe they just like humiliating the elderly. The ghost waved her hand in front of her nose as if something smelled rotten. *Those two little girls look innocent enough, but they're evil. Evil!*

"They are not," said Grace. She remembered their adorable faces while she'd read them a story. Those two darlings didn't have a mean bone in their bodies. And that was saying something considering their father, who was maliciousness incarnate, had been systematically killing them by draining their magic.

I'm more familiar with bedeviled children than you are. For instance, Betty Parris and Abigail Williams. They looked like little angels until they lost their damned minds and lied their asses off about being tormented.

"Not this again," said Grace. "You like to leave out the part where you cursing Deliverance started that whole disaster."

I know, wailed Dorcas. The witch burst into tears. *And I'm sorry, okay? I'm sorry, but it doesn't matter because I can't change the past. And I can't change the curse. And I don't want to go where the bad witches go!* With that revelation, she floated up and resumed her previous horizontal-stare-at-the-ceiling position.

Wow. Dorcas really was in a funk. She'd never seen the ghost at a loss for sarcastic, biting comebacks before. And apologies? Holy crap. It was more than a little unsettling. In order to take Dorcas' mind off her humiliation, Grace blurted, "Tabor thinks I'm his mate."

That announcement got Dorcas off her pity pot. She came down in a rush and hovered in front of Grace. *What? Are you shitting me? He said that?*

"His mom did. And if I'm honest, I'm *this close* to tackling him and ripping off his clothes."

Do you want to be mated to him?

"I just met him."

You ever been around bear shifters before? Especially Standing Bears? You could mate with him tomorrow or next year. Same difference to him. She tilted her head, her lips pursed. *Actually, he'd probably prefer it if you mated with him now instead of later.*

Grace found herself feeling woozy, so she sat down on the bed. Her face felt flushed, and her stomach churned. "I can't think about this right now. Talk about a punch in the face."

I think you mean a punch in the vagina. Dorcas grinned. *But you don't have to do jack shit. I'll push him down the stairs and break his legs. Then you can run away.*

That sounded almost like Dorcas was trying to help her. "I don't think we're at the escape stage yet," she said.

Well, let's keep it as a backup plan.

Oh, Goddess. Dorcas' version of assistance seemed pretty close to her definition of torment. Still. Grace didn't want to break the tenuous friendship building between them. Maybe "friendship" was too optimistic. But at least it was a positive vibe, and that was a first.

CHAPTER 8

"*P*lease don't leave us," begged Eden as she clung to Grace's leg. Erin had claimed one of Tabor's legs on the same premise.

"We're coming back," said Tabor. He placed his hand on top of Erin's blonde head and shared a look of worry with Grace.

They were being held hostage in the kitchen, despite constant reassurances that they'd only be gone for a couple of hours. Apparently 120 minutes was too long as far as the twins were concerned.

"I've never seen bonding this quick," said Rhoda. "How'd y'all do that?"

"It's not bonding, Mom. They're terrified. I promised to protect them."

Rhoda bent down. "My son always keeps his promises." She looked at each girl and offered a cheery smile. "They're going to return, I swear on a hive full of honeybees. And in the meanwhile, we'll make cookies."

The girls remained unconvinced, although the mention of cookies had garnered some interest.

Grace wanted to make them feel safe too. "Liz, would you retrieve two *angelica archangelica* seeds for me?"

Liz saluted. "On it, Grace." The lizard took off and she returned in a flash, using her sparkly green magic to glide up to the butcher block. She put two small seeds onto Grace's outstretched palm.

Grace swirled her finger over the seeds and chanted:

"Seeds of life
Protect from evil
Condemn strife
And any upheaval
Give them magic to wield
Against powers infernal
And create their shield
From the sacred circle."

The seeds twirled off Grace's palm, rising into the air and moving apart. Each seed began to spin in a large circle, and as it did so, verdant green stems and tiny leaves began to grow. As the crowns expanded, small yellow and green blooms emerged. After a moment, the plants stopped spinning. Grace directed one flower tiara to Eden's head and the other to Erin's.

"These are angel crowns," said Grace. "The *angelica archangelica* has amazing protection properties. So long as you wear them, nothing can harm you. You'll be safe."

The girls reluctantly loosened their grips, and each touched the other's blooming crown. "It feels tingly," they said together.

"That's the magic," said Grace.

Eden and Erin's face broke out into smiles. Then they looked at Rhoda. "Can we still make cookies?"

"Are you kidding? We're going to fill up this kitchen with every kind of cookie we can think of."

Tabor scratched his head. "I'm not sure I have all the ingredients for every kind of cookie you all can think of."

Grace laughed. "I can help there. I have a pantry full of baking supplies in my trailer. Chocolate chips, nuts, raisins, and lots of spices and natural flavorings. If you all want, Liz can show you where to find them. I even have sprinkles."

"Sprinkles," the twins said simultaneously. They jumped up and down, chanting, "Sprinkles, sprinkles, sprinkles!"

Tabor's happy smile warmed Grace to her own gooey center. Rhoda busied herself by pulling out pans, pre-heating the oven, as the girls followed Liz out to Grace's trailer. Tabor and Grace—and Dorcas—used the distraction to slip out the front door and into the dense woods.

~

How much longer are we going traipse through this ugly forest? It's humid and hot as Satan's balls. Besides, there's something weird about this place. I don't like it here.

"First of all, you can't feel temperature, so the whole Satan's balls comment is irrelevant," said Grace, though it was disturbingly accurate. "And secondly, if you don't like it here, go back to the cabin."

And leave you alone with the horny bear? No way. If he dips into your honeypot, we're never getting out of hell's cesspit.

"Right. I think you're too scared of the twins to face them by yourself."

I don't know what you're talking about. I ain't scared of nothing. Dorcas zoomed up, flowing above the tree line.

"What's wrong with your ghost?" asked Tabor. "And do I even want to know about Satan's balls?" He walked ahead, moving vines, branches, and other debris out of the way for Grace to pass through.

"She's complaining about the heat, which is stupid because she doesn't feel temperatures. She also says there something weird about this place." *And oh yeah, she mentioned you dipping into my honeypot.* Grace drew in a breath and exhaled slowly. Being outdoors always gave her both peace and energy, but not today. There was something really off about this place.

Tabor stopped and looked at her. "What you did with those seeds was incredible. I've never seen anything like it." His expression was filled with amazement. "Those plant crowns were beautiful."

"Would you like one, too?" she teased.

"Don't think I won't wear a crown of flowers that you made for me. I'll parade around, proud as a peacock shifter on mating day."

Grace laughed. Shyly, she touched his arm. "I'll keep that in mind."

Tabor met her gaze, and it amazed Grace how vulnerable the big, strong man looked in this moment. He put his hand over hers. "Maybe I can show you some of my favorite spots." He gestured around the forest with his other hand. "You know, after we figure out what's going on with Frank."

"I'd like that," she told him.

That bear wants to sow seeds, Grace. And not the kind that comes from plants. Mark my words, girl. That man wants to put a baby up in you!

Grace ignored Dorcas as she enjoyed the feel of Tabor's fingers caressing hers. Eventually, though, the bear shifter gave her hand an affectionate pat. "Frank's just down this way."

He kicked some broken limbs blocking the way, then pointed down an incline to a little church. They followed a dirt path to the chapel. Tabor helped her up the rickety stairs and then they went inside.

Thirteen ten-inch trunks twisted together to form Frank's massive center and the multitude of limbs that should've held blooms and leaves were empty. Grace knew the black spots on its trunk were disease, but she wasn't sure what kind.

Dorcas dropped down and put herself in front of Grace. *Don't go over there. Something's stinkier than hot dog shit. It's making me tingle—in all the wrong places.*

"The tree is sick," said Grace in a reasonable tone. "I'm here to make it better."

Look, witchalicious, I know you don't believe me because I've been a twatwaffle the entire time you've known me, but I'm serious. You don't owe the bear or the town or the goddamned tree. Walk away.

Grace was torn between Dorcas' concerned tone and the ghost's penchant for pranks. She looked sincere and more than a little scared, but Grace had been fooled before. She wasn't sure what to do with the new, sorta improved Dorcas. "Look, I…know you're worried about me breaking the curse. But I promise you that right now, all I want to do is see if I can heal the tree."

I remember this place, said Dorcas. *See how the floor is built around the tree? They planted the seed there. They intended for it to grow on sacred ground, to be part of the town's soul. The Bear Clan had their shaman bless the land. And Deliverance and Philip said their prayers to the Goddess. Then they built this church.*

"What happened to the town?" asked Grace. Her question was for Dorcas, but it was Tabor, standing beside her, that answered.

"We've saved journals from the settlers—and there are the oral stories passed down through the Bear Clan. It boils down to a loss of faith. Or maybe it's more like people changed their purpose. They moved away. Forgot about the magic. Let their beliefs in the otherworldly die as they embraced more modern times. It used to be that humans and parakind lived together, but somewhere along the line, humans began to fear what they didn't understand. It became necessary for us to retreat into myth and legend." He glanced at the tree. "Frank still has magic, but it used to be stronger. Think of Frank as an amplifier. It enhances your magic and your magic feeds it. Basically, it creates a circle of unending power."

"I can see why you and the Bear Clan want to keep this place protected. It's like that in Broken Heart, too. I mean, there's not a magical tree—but it's the same concept." Grace looked around. "Wouldn't it be amazing if another sanctuary like Broken Heart could be built here? A place for lost souls. Like us."

Tabor captured her gaze. "Yes," he said softly. "Like us."

As they drew closer to Frank, an overwhelming sense of foreboding overcame Grace. Dorcas wrung her hands and seemed to get more and more jittery by the second. Grace was a witch with her power attached to nature, and every-thing about the tree seemed to be in direct conflict with her magic. She glanced at Dorcas. Maybe, this one time, she should give the dead witch some credence.

If you die, I'm off to hell or somewhere worse, you nincompoop. Do you think I'd bullshit you? This tree is bad ju-ju! Dorcas' fear was palpable and it made Grace think twice about ignoring the ghost's warning.

Tabor's smile melted into a frown when he saw her expression. "What's wrong?"

"Dorcas thinks something heinous will happen if I try to help Frank."

Tabor held out his hand. "You'll be safe," he said. "I won't let anything happen to you, Grace. Hear that, Dorcas? I'll protect her."

Reassured, Grace threaded her fingers through his, and together they walked toward Frank. Dorcas followed, muttering about the follies of stupid witches and stubborn bear shifters.

Grace walked around Frank, gently touching the black patches. The tree seemed to shudder under her fingertips. Next, she poked through a pile of red leaves. Other than the fact they had fallen off the limbs, there didn't appear to be anything wrong with them.

"I've never seen this before. It appears to be some kind of fungal disease, but...I can't be sure." She bent down and brushed her fingers across the gnarled roots. "I have to get underneath it."

Tabor crossed his arms, his biceps bulging with the action. "How are we going to do that?"

She led the bear shifter around to the backside and showed him a hole that stretched from the roots to about half way up the trunk. "This morning, I looked through one of my favorite research books—*History of Ancient Trees and Their Magical Properties*."

At Tabor's puzzled look, she added, "I keep an archive of books on my computer's cloud network and I can access it through an app on my phone."

"You gotta love technology."

"It's convenient," agreed Grace. "I don't envy the days of having to use the Dewey Decimal system and card files to do research."

It was worse in the 1600s, said Dorcas. *We had one book. The Bible. That's it. That's all you ever got.*

Grace ignored Dorcas' grousing. "Frank isn't quite unique. He's one of a very few magical trees left in this world, but they all have one thing in common. They're hollow, and they open up into a cave system. We can climb inside and wiggle down the roots. Frank is probably getting its sustenance from an enchanted underground lake. That would explain how these trees are able to maintain their health and magic for so long. That might be why Deliverance chose this area. She must have known about a magical underground water supply."

"I knew there was a network of caves. There are entrances all over the place. But I didn't realize you could get access through the tree itself." Tabor gazed at the disease-infested trunk. "You think its water source might have dried up?"

"Maybe." She reached out with her magic, tugging at any thread of life she could find in Frank. A plant dying from neglect would have responded to her. Water was there, but like the tree itself, there was something putrid about it. "I think...Frank has been poisoned."

"What?" Alarmed, Tabor turned his worried gaze to the tree. "Are you sure?"

"No. That's why we need to go underground and see what's going on. I'm not saying it's an intentional poisoning. It might be that something toxic entered its food supply, or a diseased animal died in or near its water outlet." Her head spun with the possibilities. "It's all speculation, of course. That's why we need to investigate further."

"Let me go first," he said. He tried to push his massive shoulders through the opening. That didn't work, so he tried going legs first. Unsurprisingly, he didn't fit. "Maybe I should shift."

"Because a bear is so much smaller."

Tabor growled. "My bear is a lot a stronger."

Grace hid her smile. His need to protect her warmed her from head to toe. She'd never had anyone care whether she

MICHELE BARDSLEY

was in harm's way. She thought about his bear form and chuckled. "You know what happened to Pooh, right?"

"Pooh?"

She raised a brow. "How are you going to feel when your ass is hanging out of the tree because you've wedged your shoulders in? That is not an area I'd want exposed. There are all kinds of critters out here looking for warm places to hide. Are you sure you want to take that chance?"

Tabor tapped his chin, considering the merits of her advice. Did the man think he could somehow force his bulk through that space by sheer force of will? He finally conceded with a sharp nod. But then he said, "You're not going down there by yourself."

"I won't be alone." She gestured to her floating pain-in-the-ass companion and realized Tabor was watching her point at air. "Dorcas will be with me."

Don't drag me into this. I warned you. Being here is still a spectacularly idiotic move.

"She's thrilled to accompany me," said Grace. "We won't be gone long."

CHAPTER 9

"I don't like this." Tabor took Grace's hands and pulled her toward him. "Didn't you say that Dorcas told you something bad would happen? What if she's right about the negative vibe?"

Thank. You. Dorcas glared at Grace. *The bear gets it. Why don't you? Tell him the truth—that you're being an obstinate ass goblin!*

"What?" asked Tabor. He looked up as if he might actually see Dorcas. "She's talking, isn't she?"

"Yep. She says you're being a weenie." Grace tried to keep a straight face.

Weenie! Are you kidding me? If you're going to put words in my mouth then you can at least be original. Tell him I think he's a bee sucking, honey munching, furry fucking asswipe.

"Grace—"

Grace held up her hand to forestall his protest. "Please don't fight with me about this, Tabor. Yes, something nasty is happening with the tree, but you brought me here for a reason. This is my area of expertise. Let me do my job. I'll pinky-swear to be vigilant and careful."

"I'm not a weenie," Tabor grumbled.

"You are brave and strong and handsome. The fact that you want to protect me makes me feel like a queen. But I'm a witch, and I'm very good at my craft. I can handle myself."

"You think I'm handsome?" Tabor grinned.

"Maybe." A zing went straight to her girly bits. Handsome didn't even begin to cover Tabor's good looks.

"Go on. Admit it. You think I'm hot, don't you? Eden and Erin were right. You want to see my boobs."

"I already saw your boobs. And yes, I was very impressed."

Tabor gathered Grace into his embrace. "Well, I haven't seen yours." He pressed his forehead to hers. "Yet. So don't go getting yourself killed or anything."

"Because you want to see my boobs?" She considered pulling a spring break move and just yanking up her shirt.

"Because you're my mate."

"Right. You really believe that I'm your mate because we smell good to each other?"

"It's more than that. There's a primal part of shifter biology that kicks into gear when mates get within sniffing distance. I hate to say it, but I think my family was right about the honey jitters. And baby, I've got them bad for you. "

Grace's heart knocked against her ribcage. They were chest to chest. Dear Goddess. His muscles had muscles. And her nipples were so hard she was pretty sure they could carve "mine" into his flesh. "I'm not a shifter."

"Doesn't matter." Tabor's eyes were so dark, so intense, that she lost the ability to speak. He stepped closer and put his thumb on the corner of her mouth. "You are beautiful."

Okay. I'm outta here. I'd rather be eaten slowly by a troll with rancid breath rather than watch you two suck face. I'll just go wait in the scary cave. Alone.

Grace barely heard Dorcas. Butterflies danced in her belly as desire thickened her blood. Summer scents of grass, sunshine, and earth flooded her senses. She shivered, rocked to the core by the pure heat that poured through her.

"You smell like honey to me," he said softly. "I've never wanted to lick another person so much." He closed his eyes and inhaled deeply then his tongue traced her lips. "Mmm-mm." He opened his eyes, and Grace saw his desire, and beyond that, his sincerity.

"This is all so ... unexpected," said Grace. "Everything seems to be upside down and inside out."

"Yes. But us being together is a good thing." His fingers curved behind her neck, and he put his lips to hear ear. "I want you so much, Grace."

"I want you, too."

"I'm happy to hear that." Tabor bent down and pressed his mouth against hers, and Grace's doubts shattered.

~

*T*abor brushed her lips, once, twice, and moaned as her luscious mouth connected with his. He slid his arms around her waist and pulled her close, needing to hold her tightly. Why did he feel like she was going to slip away from him?

He lingered on her lips, loving their soft warmth. Goddess above! She even tasted like honey. Reluctantly, he broke their tender kiss, but only so he could enjoy other pleasures. He kissed the underside of her chin and then trailed light kisses across her jaw, stopping to nip her earlobe. To his delight, she gasped and put her arms around his neck. Her fingers delved into his hair.

With his tongue, he traced the shell of her ear, eager to give her more enjoyment. She arched, offering her neck to him, and he took the invitation. When he sampled the tender flesh in the hollow between her neck and collarbone,

Grace drew in a sharp breath, and her hands clutched his hair.

He was on the edge of taking her right here, right now. He crushed his mouth against hers. His kiss demanded more as hot need coursed through him. He plunged his tongue again and again into her mouth. He heard her soft cry of pleasure, and pure male satisfaction rushed through him. He wanted to roar. He wanted to claim her. His mate. She filled his senses so completely, his very soul felt connected to hers. All he knew or cared about for this moment was her.

Grace.

The scent that was hers alone enticed him to explore further. Through her T-shirt, he cupped her left breast. She moaned, pressing against his hand. He pinched her nipple lightly through the barrier of her lace bra. Had he ever wanted a woman so much? No, his mind cried, never. She was the only woman who stirred the mating frenzy in him. Cupping her bottom, he lifted her and rubbed his erection against the core of her femininity.

"Wait," she managed. She quivered in his arms, her eyes dark with passion. She pulled back. "I think we need to slow down."

Tabor nodded. "You're right. Besides, I don't want our first time to be here." He grinned. "Maybe our fourth or fifth time, but definitely not the first."

"Definitely not the first," she echoed.

Reluctantly, Tabor let her go. She stepped back and straightened her shirt. Her mouth was swollen from the intensity of their kiss and her long purple-gold hair slightly mussed. She was fucking adorable.

"Can I talk you out of crawling into that hole and facing goddess knows what in that cave?" he asked.

"Nope."

He sighed. "Okay. But if you're gone longer than ten

minutes, I'm coming after you even if it means yanking Frank up by the roots."

"Give me fifteen," she said. She put her palm against his cheek, her expression confident. "Don't worry, Tabor. I'll be fine."

She scuttled into the hole before he could protest again. As soon as her head disappeared, he looked at his watch.

The fifteen-minute countdown had begun.

~

*G*race climbed down the roots of the *Franklinia Magica*. Too late, she wondered how far away the ground would be once she got clear of the tangles. The darkness wrapped around her so tightly that its thick silence nearly suffocated her.

"Dorcas?"

You know that bear is going to run when he sees all those cobwebs in your v-jay-jay, right? Dorcas's irritated voice filtered through the roots. *No man wants to compete with dust and spiders when they're sexing you up.*

"I..." Grace sputtered. Then suddenly, she laughed. All these years, she'd let the shrew get under her skin, but Tabor's kiss changed her whole outlook. She felt bold and happy. Slowly, she felt her way down the bumpy twists and turns. She began to sweat and her muscles started to ache.

Finally, her feet touched the rocky floor of the cave. She stepped away from Frank, dusting off her hands. Dorcas floated nearby, arms crossed, her expression a mixture of fear and fury. Neon fuzz stripped the craggy walls, casting the cavern in an eerie green glow.

Grace looked around. Everything seemed dead. She'd never seen any plant or area so foully corrupted. Worse yet, it smelled like boiled garbage and cat piss. Ugh. "What can cause something like this?"

It's probably eboligonnaboilyourbutt, Dorcas said unhelpfully.

Grace gave the ghost an exasperated look.

Dorcas shrugged. *Don't blame me when you start bleeding out your holes.*

"Speaking of holes—why don't you shut yours?"

The witch-ghost poofed out of sight. Grace should have felt relieved to be rid of Dorcas for a moment, but instead, she felt apprehensive. Bad company was better than no company on a mission like this.

The odd light allowed her to see that the largest root, as big around as a wooden barrel. It looked as diseased as the rest of Frank.

Dorcas re-appeared. *I still think we should hightail it out of here before something horrible happens.*

"If you feel that strongly about it," said Grace, "then go. You don't have to stick around."

Yes, I do. If you get your dumb ass killed then I'm a goner, too. She nodded toward the left. *That big root goes all the way down to the next cave.*

"Did you follow it to the end?"

Hell, no. You need to hurry your witchy-self up, missy. This place gives me the creeps.

"It does me, too." Grace indulged her curiosity about the fuzzy green stuff on the cave walls. It looked alive, but it didn't *feel* alive. She went in for a closer look.

"Bioluminescent fungi," she said. "Fascinating."

Yeah, it's a real thrill, all right. Let's go already.

They followed the huge root until it curved to the right, into a bigger cavern. More of the glowing fungi covered the walls. Grace felt the magic of this place. Ancient. Powerful.

Damaged. Underneath the decay, she could detect the once pure sorcery.

The root went straight into a large body of water.

The hair on the back of Grace's neck stood straight up, and she knew Dorcas was right. A putrid presence coated the whole area. Yet, here they were, being bad asses. Black dross floating on top of what had no doubt once been a gorgeous, crystal clear lake. Grace could almost see it in her mind's eye. But now it was, as she had suspected, poisoned.

Dorcas sailed upward and circled around the lake. She returned, looking sick to her stomach. *Somebody took a major dump all over this area. That black crud is gonna leave a skid mark on nature's ass.*

Grace knelt at the edge of the lake and put her hand over the inky substance. She sent out her magic, trying to connect with whatever this was so she could either heal it or kill it.

The scuzzy crap didn't like her poking at it. It almost felt like the poison was using her conjuration as a tether, slithering toward her and destroying her magic as it went.

She cut the connection and jumped to her feet. Plants couldn't be evil, right? Real evil required a soul. She stared at the tarry surface of the lake. This crap was everywhere. If she couldn't figure out what it was and how to remove it, Frank would die.

Holy shitballs! It's Bigfoot or Swamp Thing. No! It's the Creature from the Black Lagoon! Someone tied Nessie's rotting corpse to a tar pit and let it putrefy before bringing it back to life! The ghost witch pointed behind Grace.

Grace turned and saw a huge, greasy, pile of mire rise and trudge across the lake's morass. Unlike Dorcas, it took Grace precious seconds to realize it was a monster of epic proportions. The thing was Godzilla-sized, or at least it felt that way as it splashed across the water and headed toward the shore.

Dorcas whacked Grace on the back of the head with a spongy, fetid piece of driftwood. *Run, you moron!*

Grace raced from the lake's cave and into the larger cavern. She could hear the thing slishing behind her. It was fast for a lumbering, feculent giant. As soon as she got to Frank's massive roots, she began her desperate climb upward.

Hurry, yelled Dorcas. *Get your good-for-nothing ass movii-iiiiing!*

Adrenaline shot through Grace as she thought about what was behind her. What the hell was that thing? A plant? A humanoid? A supernatural being?

As she wiggled through the curling roots, she could see the light from the tree's entry point. Tabor poked his head through. "Grace!"

Heart pounding, hands sweating, and muscles aching, she kept going. Tabor reached out a hand. "You're almost there."

She reached for Tabor.

He was just inches away.

A horrible feeling shuddered through her and then she felt the thing grab her leg and pull. She screamed.

Desperation swept across Tabor's face as he swiped at her hand, and she stretched out her fingers, barely making contact with his palm.

"Grace!"

The slimy creature yanked her down.

And then she was sliding down the trunk, away from Tabor.

Away from safety.

CHAPTER 10

*A*gitated, Dorcas zipped above Grace's head. The ghost's eyes widened in fear and horror. That's when Grace realized she was in way worse trouble that she first believed.

The thing that had clamped onto her leg yanked her down. She scraped against the scabrous bark, her face banging against the knots and curves.

Then she was flat on the cave floor, pinned by the walking trash pile. Oh, Goddess. The damn thing had a face, and…it was smiling. The beast stood over her, his piggish red eyes glowing with malice. It reached out a hand—or its version of a hand. One greasy tendril curled out of its finger and twisted toward her.

She realized with the clarity of the probably-gonna-die that this creature siphoned magic and replaced it with its poison. Her stomach dropped as panic scurried through her. What it'd been doing to Frank, it wanted to do to her.

Dorcas flew through the monster and screamed, *Cowabunga, motherfucker!* When she came through the other side, she was spitting all over the place. *Yuck. I got supernat-*

ural butt nuggets in my mouth. She looked over her shoulder. *Are we seriously getting our asses kicked by a piece of walking shit?*

"Yeah," Grace shouted. "You need to find a way in for Tabor and get him here."

What am I? Lassie?

"You want me to get my face eaten off by Mr. Personality over here?"

Fine! I'm going! Try not to let him kill you before I get back with the big tub 'o fur, all right? She popped out of the cave.

Grace drew on her magic. Blue flames lit up her arms as she called for water. A large water ball formed in her hands. She used all her might to throw it at the beast above her. It hit the creature, but it had the force of a whiffle ball. What could she do next? The place was so oily and gassy, fire magic might or might not kill her attacker, but it would certainly barbeque her and Frank's roots in the process. She tried lightning next. The bolt hit the ginormous turd and sizzled.

He rubbed his belly. "That tingled in a good way, witch."

Grace's eyes widened. It spoke! "What do you want?"

"I want to live, you greedy spellcaster."

Grace could feel the sickness of his magic tainting her own. She called out a spell to try to disseminate the creature. A pile of slop hit her in the mouth. *Oh, gross, gross, gross!*

"None of that, witch! The tree has been dinner, but you are the perfect dessert. I can dine on your essence."

Grace spit out the oily gunk that tasted like rotten spinach and had the consistency of lumpy pudding. Blech. Her gag reflex kicked in, and she coughed out the sludge. "Dude. Consider a spa day. You're disgusting."

"Try to cast another spell, and you'll get more than that shoved in your mouth."

"Oh, please. You call that a threat? Maybe you should go back to villain school." She glanced round the large cavern.

She couldn't defeat him on her own, and she wasn't going to let him near Frank—or allow his ugly ass anywhere near the surface. Tabor could probably crush this prick flat in less than a minute. But until he got here, she had to distract Poopy McPoopPants. "Why are you killing Frank? What did it ever to do you?"

"It exists." He held out his muddy hand, and Grace felt him pull the energy right out of her. A greenish-gold light snaked out of her abdomen and pierced his palm. He put up his other hand, and a noxious stream of black smoke broke through his skin and slithered into her mouth. As he took the good from her and shoved in the bad, his corrupt magic made nausea roil in her stomach.

Grace felt herself weakening.

"You are delicious." His red eyes sparkled with sick excitement. "I have been too long in the underworld." He flexed his gloppy fists. "Too long slithering in the dark!"

"Stop it, Narn!" yelled a man's deep voice. "You can't kill her."

Grace's head felt fuzzy. It was getting difficult to form coherent thoughts. She turned toward the male voice and saw a tall man pressed into the cavern wall. He was covered head-to-toe in brownish-green goop. His face was smeared with the sludge, but he could still see and talk.

The creature frowned. It was clear he didn't appreciate Wall Dude's contribution to their conversation.

"I'm Lucas Dark," said the man. "And Narn escaped from the underworld. He's not supposed to be here."

"I am, too!" Narn pumped up the process of trading her magic with his toxic drudge. Her skin turned black, and she swore she could feel her lungs shrinking.

"Narn! Stop it!"

"I won't go back to the underworld."

The ethereal place within her where she tapped into her

creator gifts cracked open, and he began to drain her in earnest. Tears leaked from Grace's eyes as she thought of Tabor. Finally, she'd found a man who wanted to be with her, love her, despite her curse, and she wasn't going to survive to mate with him.

As her peripheral vision dimmed, she did something she never thought she'd do—pray for Dorcas to help her. *Hurry, you old bitty. Hurry, before...*

Everything went black.

∾

abor slammed his palm against the tree. How the fuck was he supposed to get to Grace? His heart raced as fear poured over him, chilling him to the bone. *Think, Tabor.* The nearest cave entrance was miles away. Even if he got there quickly, he wouldn't have any idea how to get to Grace. The caverns were endless. It was easy to get lost in all the twists and turns.

Something hard slammed into the back of his head. "Ow!" He turned around and saw a rock hovering near his knees. "Who threw that?"

The rock dropped onto his foot. He yelped and hopped up on one leg. Then he watched a twig rise from the ground. It tipped up and then started scraping on the dirt-filled floor. Then he realized what was happening. "Dorcas?"

The stick jabbed at the dirt and spelled out: Yes. Moron.

"Where's Grace?"

Dorcas, or so he assumed, scratched away the first note and scribbled a second: Follow me.

"How am I supposed to do that?" he asked. "I can't see you."

Underneath "Follow me" Dorcas wrote: U R Stupid.

"Quit fucking around, Dorcas."

The thin branch whipped through the air and smacked him on the ass.

"Shit!" The whack really stung. Then the stick, moving up and down like a baton, started moving away from Frank and out of the church.

Tabor didn't know what Dorcas' intentions were, but he had to believe she was leading him to Grace. He figured his second form would be more useful when it came to rescuing the witch. He shifted into his bear before lopping behind the bobbing sprig. *Hang on, Grace!*

Dorcas led him down an embankment. When it rained hard, this channel filled up with water. Right now, it was dry, which turned out to be a good thing. The stick pointed at a stack of broken limbs and forest debris. As a bear, it took maybe 3.5 seconds for him to destroy the blockage and enter the cave.

He hadn't known about this little passage, and he was grateful the ghost had somehow discovered it. Once again, the twig bobbed in front of him. The cave walls were dotted with glowing green plants, which offered enough light to navigate through the tunnels. After what felt like a never-ending maze, the cave tunnels opened into a large open area.

Then he saw Grace.

And the creature crouched over her.

"Stop it, Narn! I mean it!" someone shouted.

Tabor glanced at the man stuck in the wall like Han Solo frozen in carbonite and growled at him.

"Look, you better stop him," the guy said to Tabor. "Narn is not messing around. He will suck her dry and finish off the tree after. Then this world will really be in for it."

Tabor watched as the ugly son-of-a-bitch sucked in Grace's beautiful green-gold magic. The color of plants. Of life. Of her. His mate. Worse yet, the creature was emitting a noxious black cloud that swirled into Grace's mouth.

Tabor roared and galloped toward the monster. He reared up on his hind legs and struck the decaying piece of shit full on in the chest. It rolled off Grace, its grin dripping black poison as it got to its feet. It rushed Tabor, but he caught the stinky bastard between his paws and began to squeeze. It squealed and screamed. Tabor was worried sick about Grace and furious this thing had hurt her. Tabor swung the slippery piece of trash out and let go, slamming it as hard as he could against the cave wall. The creature slid down to the ground and lay still.

Within moments, Tabor shifted back into his human form and hurried to kneel by Grace's side. She looked pale— as if every drop of blood had been drained from her. Her green eyes were filled with pain and her breathing turned thready. He was losing her.

He stroked her hair. His voice choked as he said, "Stay with me, Grace. Stay with me."

She offered one last smile and then released her final breath.

~

*L*iz sat on the couch between Eden and Erin watching *Scooby Doo and the Witch's Ghost* as they ate chocolate-chip cookies. Pain slammed into her so hard she wretched to her feet, her frill opening to its full display. "Something's wrong with Grace," she whispered.

Rhoda remained in the kitchen cleaning up after the baking frenzy. Liz could hear her on the phone, talking to a friend about a town barbecue for the Fourth of July. "Gotta go, mates. Grace needs me."

"She needs us, too," said the girls together. Then they put their hands on Liz and all three of them poofed out of the living room.

~

*D*orcas rarely used magic. It drained her energy and besides, gathering magic as a ghost was a thousand times harder. All the same, she wasn't going to let his bear-ass-ness tend to Grace while he was naked. She wrapped him in a robe, the best she could do given her limited abilities. It about wore her out, too. One minute Dorcas was hovering above Grace watching Tabor pull the witch onto his lap while he sobbed and the next she was in an empty space.

She looked around and saw nothing. Wherever this was had no walls, no doors, no anything. It was just a great big endless sea of white.

"Dorcas." She whirled around and saw Deliverance Fucking Hobbs gliding in her direction. She looked about the same as she had the last time Dorcas had seen her alive. Deliverance had gotten old by actual living out her full life. Graying brown hair poked out from white bonnet, an austere indigo dress covered her stick-like body, and she wore black leather buckle shoes. The only thing different was the glittering gold key on a chain around her neck.

"That's what you died in? Seriously?"

"It wasn't like I could head on down Sacs Fifth Avenue," said Deliverance. She rolled her eyes. "You haven't changed in four-hundred-years.

"Neither have you." Deliverance offered a thin smile. "How are you?"

"How am I? *I'm dead.* Where the hell are we?"

"Think of it as a waiting room."

"Wait. Did Grace die?"

Deliverance tilted her head. "Would you care if she did?"

"Of course I would," snapped Dorcas. "She's too young to

pass away. She got this bear shifter and these two little brats she kinda likes. And what would Liz do without her?"

\ Deliverance spread out her hands in supplication. "I'm sorry, Dorcas. There's really nothing I can do. You're here because Grace will permanently depart the earthly plane very soon. It's time for you to move on to the next realm."

"You can take the next realm and shove it up your puckered asshole." Dorcas pointed at her. "You get me back to Grace, and you do it now."

"Same old bossy bitch." Deliverance drew herself up in the same snooty way Dorcas remembered and said, "You always think the rules don't apply to you."

"Because they don't." Dorcas' gaze was once again drawn to the gold key. "What is that?"

"I'm a steward here. This allows me to move between worlds so I can help souls transition."

"Can you use it to go back to Earth?"

"I suppose. But nobody goes back, Dorcas. If you leave this realm and return to Earth, you'll be stuck there forever. You don't get a second chance to die."

"Dying's overrated." Dorcas reached over and yanked the chain off Deliverance's neck. The minute she held the key in her hand, a blue and green door appeared.

"Give that back!" yelled Deliverance. "Dorcas, don't you dare step through that door!"

Dorcas tossed the key at Deliverance, who caught it easily. Then she flipped her nemesis the bird and dove through the door.

CHAPTER 11

When Dorcas arrived back in the cave, she saw Tabor, the twins from hell, and Liz surrounding the limp body of Grace. She rushed forward and lowered herself in the middle of the circle.

Grace lay on the ground, pale from the creature's attack. Dorcas couldn't believe that witch had the nerve to die on her. She reached down and smacked her cheek. *Hey, lazy bones, wake up.*

"She's not dead," said Eden. She sat down and placed her arm on Grace's shoulder.

"If we help her, she'll live." Erin sat next to her sister and put her hand on Grace's hip. Dorcas saw the tears in Liz's eyes.

Don't just sit there, you scaly bitch. Do something.

"I feel empty," said Liz. "Our connection is gone. She's not there, Dorcas."

Well, you might as well give the fuck up then, right?

Liz sniffled. "Shut up." She crawled onto Grace's chest and lay down. On the other side of Grace sat Tabor. He looked shell-shocked.

Hey. Little girls. Tell Tabor to suck it up. Then tell him he has to bring that shit pile over here.

Eden and Erin conveyed the message.

"Dorcas, are you sure you know what you're doing?" asked Liz.

Hell, no, but I've never let that stop me.

Once the twins had repeated her words, Tabor gently put Grace on the ground. He rose to his feet and traipsed to the prone creature. Even from here, Dorcas could smell the foulness of the ugly thing. Much to Dorcas' surprise and disgust, the creature still lived. She wanted to punch a hole in it and pull out its guts.

Dorcas watched Tabor drop the thing near Grace. "Now what?"

Girls, put one of your hands on Slime Boy and the other on Grace. Tell Tabor to do it, too. Grace's going to need all the life force she can get.

Once everyone was settled, Dorcas looked at the girls. *Say this spell:*

What was lost
Must now be gained
What was wild
Must now be tamed
Help us now to conquer fear
Return to us our sister dear

The girls and Liz repeated the spell. Everybody kept still and quiet waiting for the magic to work. Dorcas prayed harder than she ever had in her life—or death, for that matter—that the Goddess would return Grace to life.

Nothing happened.

Liz broke the silence first with her sobs. The kids looked

at Dorcas, their gazes filled with sadness. And Tabor—poor bear shifter—held on to Grace's hand tightly. He didn't want to let her go.

Nobody in this cave wanted Grace to leave.

"Maybe I can help."

Dorcas turned to the wall and noticed there was a man stuck inside it. *Who the fuck are you?*

"Lucas Dark."

You can see me?

"I was born in the underworld. My dad is Charon. It's kinda my thing."

"Is that piece of shit your thing?" asked Tabor.

"No. Well, sorta. He belongs to the underworld. He escaped, and he's been siphoning the magic here so he can stay. I was supposed to come here and stop him."

Well, you really suck at your job, said Dorcas.

"Holy Goddess!" yelled a female voice. "What is that smell? Did someone shit themselves?"

Dorcas whirled and saw Zerina, dressed in a white frilled top, a checkered white-and-blue mini-skirt, thigh-high white stockings, and glittery blue high-tops. "Rhoda called me in panic. Said everyone disappeared. Lucky for me I have fairy GPS." She took in the scene. "Looks like I got here just in time."

Wrong, you asstwit! She's dead. Your timing sucks.

Zerina gagged. "Can you smell that? I can taste it—that's how rank it is."

The source of the smell regained consciousness and rose to its sloppy feet. Its red eyes had nothing but hatred in them as it stepped toward the group, growling.

"Aaaaaaahhhh!" screamed Zerina. "What the hell is going on?"

"If someone would *please let me the fuck down*, I can help."

Zerina turned toward Lucas. "If you don't, whoever-the-fuck-you-are, I will wear your guts for garters." She aimed her palms toward the wall and melted it. Lucas slid out of the muck and spun across the mossy cavern floor.

"Finally." He stood and shook off the mud. "This is over, Narn." He lifted a hand and said, *"Ad mortem."*

Narn screamed, lurched forward, and then melted into a stinky pile of muck.

Zerina bent at the waist, inhaling deep breaths, probably so she wouldn't yark. "Shit around here is getting so fucking weird. And I live in Broken Heart, the center of Universe Weird."

"Look at that," said Tabor.

Swirling above them was a huge pool of gold and green magic. The power of it was immense. Even Dorcas could feel it pulse with life. This was good magic. One of health and love and happiness.

"I'll need everyone to make this work," said Lucas. "Surround Grace, put your hands on her, think positive thoughts, and repeat after me:

"Power above
Witch below
Goddess of love
Pure of soul
Grant dominion now
To the one you adore
She becomes the bough
She becomes the core
The protector of secrets
The guardian of truth
The newest priestess
The witches' sooth

If dear Goddess you agree
Then as of now, so mote it be."

The magic swirling above them reformed into a tornado of green and gold light. The funnel swirled toward Grace and dove inside her. The force of the impact blew everyone backward.

The brilliant light was blinding.

Then it disappeared.

All that was left was Grace. She awoke and sat up. Her hair was now a mossy green and her eyes glowed gold with an otherworldly power.

"What's going on?" she asked. Tabor helped her to feet.

"The only way to save you and the tree was to combine your energies," said Lucas. "What was the *Franklinia Magica*... is now you."

Grace tilted her head. "Oh. And who are you?"

He's Lucas Dark, pronounced Dorcas, who had a suspiciously wet glint in her eyes, *and he saved your ass, so he's okay in my book.*

Tabor took Grace into his arms and kissed her soundly. "Never do that again."

❧

*T*wo *days later...*
"We have the cabin to ourselves. Even Dorcas is giving us privacy," said Tabor.

He lay in the huge king-sized mattress next to her, deliciously naked. She wasn't wearing a stitch of clothing, either. *All the better to ravish you with, m'dear,* Grace thought.

She smiled, feeling utterly amazing. Becoming the *Franklinia Magica* wasn't exactly a walk in the park. She was still getting used to her new powers, not to mention her new hairstyle. Tabor had been with her every step of the way.

"I'm glad the girls are staying with us," she said. "We really can protect them the best."

"Between a bear shifter, a kick-ass witch, an ornery familiar, and a foul-mouthed ghost—yeah, I think we're the best bet for Eden and Erin."

"Damn skippy." She grinned. "Well, maybe not the foul-mouthed ghost."

After she awoke from the transformation, Grace knew two things: She'd found her purpose. And she'd found her mate.

Now, it was time to pledge their lives, and their love, to each other.

Tabor lay on his side and Grace lay on her back. Trembling with unquenchable desire, she stared at him. He studied her with slow deliberation, touching her with his gaze before even laying a finger on her. As his brown eyes wandered down the curve of her neck to her aching breasts, her nipples hardened and sent tingles of pleasure straight to her groin. She clenched her hands into fists as he continued his perusal down to the vee of her thighs, then her legs. Even her feet didn't escape the heat of his gaze.

"You're beautiful," he whispered. "My mate."

She had no words—couldn't find words to describe how she felt. Without touching her, he had made white-hot passion burn through her. With his thumb, he pressed against the throbbing nub between her thighs. She gasped at the sudden touch and his uncanny accuracy. He stroked her as he leaned down. She felt his breath on her neck, knew his mouth was only inches away. The smell of fresh-cut grass and sun-warmed soil swirled around her, making her hotter than ever.

"Touch me, Tabor."

"I will," he whispered, "Believe me, I will." He lifted her hair and brushed his lips across her neck. Then his hands glided down her arm to her abdomen. As he skimmed her flesh she gasped, reveling in sweet touches of his fingertips. She felt his arousal against her thigh, and she reached down to grip his shaft. A thrill of feminine power shot through her when he groaned. His hand slid over her hip and trailed up her ribcage. He stroked the undersides of her breasts.

Tabor's fingers worked a sensual magic on her breasts with long, tormenting touches. Finally, oh finally, he cupped one breast, his palm pushing against her distended nipples. "Grace, let me love you."

Her only connection to the world was Tabor. He moved on top of her and gently pinched her nipples, sending shards of exquisite pleasure to pierce her very core. "Tabor," she moaned.

Her breasts ached to be touched. However, Tabor didn't touch her with his hands again, instead she felt the warm wetness of his mouth as his lips closed over one nipple. She moaned and arched, offering him as much as he could take. His tongue laved her tingling flesh until she was gasping, her hands reaching until she found his shoulders. He released her breast and turned to the other one. Once again, his mouth pleasured her until hunger coiled hot and tight in the center of her being.

His hands replaced his mouth, cupping them firmly, fingertips caressing the taut peaks.

"Look, Grace," Tabor said, "Look at our passion."

Grace looked down. Tabor's brown hands were stark against the white of her breasts. She fit him perfectly, her nipples responding to every touch. Fierce hunger swirled through her as she watched Tabor's tender attentions. She reached up and touched the dark brown hair on his chest. It felt like wisps of silk under her exploring fingertips. This felt so right. So good. The need he had awakened in her made her bold. She met his half-lidded gaze.

"What about you?" she asked, touching his erection. She trailed a finger over the ridge. She felt him jerk under her touch.

She pressed closer, forcing his hands to drop from her breasts, and rubbed against his chest. She surprised Tabor by pushing him onto the bed and covering him with her own body. Leaning forward, she nibbled his shoulder, trailing her lips up his neck. Then she sprinkled kisses across his chest, flicking her tongue against one of his flat nipples. It pebbled against her lips and she lightly nipped him.

"Grace?"

"Hmmm?"

"Did I mention how strong the mating frenzy was?"

She licked his nipple again and wrapped her fingers around his length. "I remember something to that effect," she murmured. God, he felt so good. His length filled her palm, hot and hard as she stroked it from tip to base.

When she encircled the tip of his erection with one finger, his body shuddered.

"Grace?" His voice sounded choked. "I don't know how long I can keep my bear from roaring and claiming you."

She didn't answer him. Instead she cupped his buttocks, loving the touch of the firm, rounded flesh, and then she got on her knees and helped him untangle the shorts from his feet. She stroked the soft, dark hair on his legs; reached up to touch his hips. Exulting in this power Tabor had given her, she looked up at him. She kept eye contact as she put her lips on his hardness and sucked him into her mouth.

"That's all I can take, witch," he growled.

He grabbed her elbows and pulled her up. As his lips crushed hers, he held her tightly.

His tongue plundered her mouth over and over while he

rubbed his hardness against the tightening nub of her core. Grace thrust her hands into his hair, reveling in his possession because she knew that in these moments, she possessed him as well.

"Tabor," she breathed. "Tabor."

She had no time to think, to protest when he rolled her over onto her back. He pressed hot kisses down her neck, into the hollow that sent a thousand shivers through her body. He worshiped her with his hands and mouth; licking her shoulder, stroking her arm, sucking her nipple. His hands skimmed her stomach and hips and then his fingers found the aching place hidden between her thighs.

She pushed against his hand as his long fingers stoked a fire that spread flames through every inch of her flesh. His mouth closed over her nipple. She cried out from the sheer ecstasy. He kissed her, his tongue keeping rhythm with his probing finger. She reached down and grasped his member.

"Goddess, Grace. I can't wait another second."

"Then don't." She wrapped her legs around him. With a hoarse cry, he thrust inside her.

"Yes," cried Grace. "So much yes."

He pulled her arms above her head and held them there with one hand. His impassioned gaze snagged hers, and she felt something within her shift. Give in. Become one. With him. Her mate.

"More," she demanded.

He moaned, his hot breath fanning her ear. His scent was so earthy, so male. She breathed it in as she bucked against him, drawing him into her deeply. His flesh filled hers over and over again.

His breathing was harsh, and his chest heaved against hers. "Grace. Damn it."

Joy surged through her as Tabor let go of his control. She tightened her legs around him and met him with her hips. A growl unleashed from him, and he sank his teeth into her breast.

The explosion of bliss caught her off guard. She felt magic as Tabor claimed her fully, his bite the same as a wedding ring. As a honeymoon. As his heart.

A tight aching need spiraled unendingly through her. She cried out, digging her nails into Tabor's muscled back. She pulsated against his hardness, waves of pleasure rolling over her. Tabor rose above her and thrust deeply. His groan of completion shot prickles of heat dancing among the remnants of bliss as he emptied himself inside her.

Are you two ass knuckles done yet? I'm stuck with the twins from hell, you know. They changed my clothes again. Liz thinks it's funny and keeps giving them suggestions. Bear boy's mother is no help at all, mostly because she can't see me. I need someone on my side.

Grace rolled her eyes and sat up in bed. "Dorcas, couldn't you have waited another five minutes? I was hoping for post-coital cuddles."

Dorcas was having none of it. She pointed at herself. *Do you see? I'm dressed like Little Miss Muffet. See this fucking bonnet? It looks like it belongs on an infant. I hate wearing knickers. Especially lacy ones that itch. Grace, make them stop.*

Grace rolled her eyes. "We agreed that you would try to be more…well, less you, if you wanted to stay. So, you're just gonna have to suck it up. And no, you can't get revenge on five-year-olds."

Fine! Take all my fun away. She paused. *What about the lizard?*

"You can try. Liz will probably whoop your ass, though."

Dorcas' gaze moved along Tabor's muscled stomach. The ghost licked her lips. *Wow. He's built.* She glanced at his face. *What's wrong with your boyfriend?*

"Husband," corrected Grace. She looked at Tabor and saw

that he'd turned bone-white. And he appeared to be staring right at Dorcas.

Concerned, Grace touched his arm. "Are you okay?"

"I can see her," he said. "I can see Dorcas."

Hot damn! Dorcas flew around the room, cackling. *Welcome to hell, furry butt. Glad you're part of the family.*

EPILOGUE

Three months later...

Grace stood in the middle of the new downtown, and smiled. Between her newly acquired magic, Zerina's somewhat dubious contributions—including the new Fashion by Zerina store next to Rhoda's Southern Sweets Café, Lucas Dark's unusual protections, and the sweat equity of Tabor, there was the beginning of a town. A sanctuary for the magically inclined.

"So, Lost Souls, huh?" asked Tabor curled an arm around her shoulder. "I like it."

"I do, too." Grace leaned against him, and took it all in. "I think it's perfect."

Ready for the next Lost Souls & Broken Hearts adventure? Read on for a sneak peek of *Peace in the Valley*!

PEACE IN THE VALLEY

AN EXTENDED SNEAK PEEK AT LOST SOULS & BROKEN HEARTS #2

PROLOGUE

Once upon a time in the small fairy kingdom of Gallia...

The sweet fairy-witch baby, Peace Elaine Crawford, lay in her elaborately decorated cradle, swaddled in glittery pink cloth, her green eyes as bright as emeralds.

Fairy Queen Skye and her warlock husband Jeremiah Crawford stood next to the bassinet of their one-month-old daughter, accepting the gifts and congratulations from Gallia's citizens. The formal presentation to the kingdom of the fairy queen's firstborn was a royal tradition. Indeed, the castle's massive ballroom had been decorated in silvers and pinks, magic glittering the air. The buffet tables were laden with decadent food and plentiful desserts—and of course, bubbling fountains of fairy wine.

Finally, it was time for the child's fairy godmothers, Gretta, Dretta, and Tretta, to bestow their gifts. The women had been godmothers to all royal firstborns for the last thousand years—and Peace would be their last godchild. It was time for the elderly fairies to hang up their wands and retire to the Elysian Fields Home for Senior Godmothers, located in the Underworld.

As they lifted their hands over the cooing infant, their final wish hovering on their lips, a cold, bitter wind blew through the ballroom, ripping decorations, knocking over tables and people, and dousing all the magic. Just steps away from the newborn's cradle, a dark purple cloud arose.

After the magical fog disappeared, a tall woman dressed in purple robes, her face thin and sharp, her obsidian eyes lifeless, and her hair as black as a priest's sins, stepped forward.

"Eartha," said Queen Skye. "You are not allowed here."

"Here?" scoffed Eartha. "In the kingdom and castle that you stole from me?" Her low chuckle chilled everyone in the room. "I am the eldest. This kingdom should be mine."

"You made your choice," said Skye, "when you accepted evil into your heart and killed our parents. You should be grateful you were only banished from the fairy realm."

"I wouldn't say I accepted evil into my heart, but I did let him into my bed." Eartha smirked. "You're a child compared to me, Skye. I've spent my entire life gathering power. I am stronger than you—I am better than you." Eartha grimaced. "This is my life you have taken. And if I can't have it…neither can you."

Eartha lifted her arms, palms out. Black and purple magic twined together and blasted into the room. Screams filled the air as the hideous sorcery wrapped around the guests.

"Fare thee well to my traitorous sister, you fool
"Good-bye to the people under your rule
"So long to the kingdom that you serve as queen
"As I take from you and yours every damned thing."

As the evil spell took form, people began to disappear.

The castle, the lands and the villages, faded into nothingness. Not even the rolling green hills and verdant forests survived the magical desecration.

Skye and Jeremiah cast their own spells, but it was too late to do more than launch a protection bubble. The black magic continued to erase Gallia and all who lived in it...until only the queen, her husband, the fairy godmothers, and the babe remained.

Eartha snapped her fingers and the protection bubble popped. She pointed a finger at the cradle, but Skye launched herself toward her sister. The purple lightning bolt meant to destroy Peace hit her mother instead.

"No!" Jeremiah caught his wife as she fell. Her breaths were shallow, her eyes filled with pain.

"I am not without mercy," said Eartha, her voice filled with vitriol. "Die with your true love." Jeremiah lifted his arm and muttered a spell. White light met the dark of Eartha's terrible magic—and was no match.

Only dark magic could defeat dark magic.

As Skye took her final breath, Eartha struck down Jeremiah, and he collapsed against his wife.

Cackling, Eartha turned toward the godmothers and the infant.

"You can't save her," hissed Eartha. "Death to the babe!" A noxious purple cloud issued from her palm and smoked toward the infant. The magic took its hold, and Eartha smiled, her black heart rejoicing.

Then she watched in horror as the fairy godmothers clasped hands and created a circle around the cradle. The bright pink and purple and blue lights of their magic blended together. The godmothers gave every bit of magic and life force they had left to give to Peace. As their magic and lives drained, their bodies turned gray and gaunt.

Eartha refused to let the old hags win. She lifted her

hands, calling on her dark magic with every intention of obliterating them.

In the blink of an eye, they disappeared.

Her final act of vengeance denied, Eartha screamed—and the sound of her hatred echoed throughout the entire fairy world.

CHAPTER ONE

Lost Souls, Arkansas

Lucas Dark slipped through the tall gates made up of blackened and gnarled bones—and raced across the obsidian sand toward the gleaming silver water of the River Styx.

The Underworld had its own devastating beauty, one he'd admired as a child growing up on the banks of Styx. Even now, the stark splendor was breathtaking. He'd never been afraid of his birthplace, despite its terrifying reputation among mortals.

But now ... the fear grew in him like cold slithering vines, squeezing his heart and his lungs.

I'm not too late.

I'm not too late.

As he drew closer to the barren shore, he saw his father Charon help the beautiful redhead into the bone-white gondola.

"Dad!" he screamed.

Charon, dressed in gray robes, a cowled hood drawn over to hide his face, shook his head.

"No! Stop!"

The woman looked over her shoulder, her expression one of sad resolve. That desolation struck him to the core. She turned her back toward him and sat down, facing the argent water. He knew they would not cross to the other side to the entrance of the Elysian Fields. No. They would head downstream, toward the tributary that led to the River Hypnos. There, she would wander the shore with no memory of who she was or the life she had lived. Or of him.

I'm not too late.

Lucas realized he'd been running as fast as he could, but now he was stuck in one place, feet digging into the hot silt, chest heaving with exertion.

His father used the oar to push the creaking boat away from the shore.

Lucas opened his mouth to scream his protest, yet no words issued forth.

Pinned into place, helpless, he watched his father direct the boat down the river—taking away the other half of his soul.

~

*L*ucas bolted upright, drenched in sweat. He took several steady breaths and attempted to calm the frantic beating of his heart.

For the last seven nights he dreamed of the redhead with the gold-green eyes and the sad expression. He pressed his fingers against his temples, frustration curling through him. Dream portents were not his specialty and all attempts to figure out the meaning of the nightmare had proven inadequate.

He felt connected to the woman. Like ... like she really was his other half. Lucas rubbed a hand through his short black hair. How was it possible to know someone he'd never met? Hell, who probably didn't even exist except in his imagination?

Maybe he needed a consultation with his mother. Her gentle manner and caring nature was nearly always soothing. That unique kindness was part of her healing gift. She was the opposite of Dad. Charon tended to be brusque and no-nonsense with mortals and immortals alike. Dad needed

Mom's softness, her sweet benevolence to counter his practical nature and rough edges.

Lucas shook off his thoughts. Not for the first time he wished he could call Mom on a cell phone. Technology didn't work in the Underworld—not that anyone would want to put cell towers on the silty shores of the River Styx. Dad would hate that. Besides, Cerberus would just knock them over and gnaw on 'em like chewies.

Sighing, Lucas lay back down and pulled the covers up to his chin. But no matter how much he tried, he couldn't go back to sleep.

And he couldn't forget about the mystery woman who haunted his waking hours, too.

Was she real?

~

Broken Heart, Oklahoma

"*Y*ou should wear a dress." Dretta's rheumy blue gaze appraised Peace Crawford's jeans and the navy-blue T-shirt emblazoned with "I crochet so I don't kill people." She frowned as she studied Peace's bright green Converses. "Why do you insist on wearing those shoes?"

"Because they're comfortable. And not high heels." Peace pulled her wavy red hair into a ponytail and whispered a spell to keep it that way. "Let's not forget the sad tale of the Heels of Regret." Peace spread out her hands. "A cocktail party. A marble staircase. And the stilettos from hell."

"Well, it's not like you had to walk around with that broken ankle. Zerina fixed that right up for you," said Dretta.

Peace remembered her emergency trip to Zerina's house. Ugh. Still, she had the fairy to thank for sending her Lucas

Dark's direction. It was Zerina's suggestion that the necromancer might be able to help.

"Now there's a fairy who knows fashion. You could ask her for some tips," said Dretta.

"No way. Don't you remember? She laughed the entire time she healed my ankle. And then she stole my heels. That woman has a serious addiction to Prada."

"Forget about the shoes." Tretta she shuffled around her sister. She only had one eye and wore a sparkly blue eyepatch over the other desiccated socket. "What you need is a leisure suit. Red plaid with a white belt."

"She's not going to a 1970s disco." Gretta pushed her way between her sisters and pointed a gnarled gray finger at her godchild. "Ignore them. They wouldn't know fashion if they tripped over it. What you need, Peace, is low-cut blouse to show off your boobs."

"I'm not changing clothes." Peace loved her zombie godmothers, she really did. But they were not exactly fashion icons. Her godmothers were dressed in tracksuits—Dretta in purple, Tretta in blue, and Gretta in pink. Add to that bright white orthopedic shoes, and you had the opposite of stylish. So, Peace was going to ignore their clothing advice and shelve it right next to their dating advice. Not that she needed opinions about her love life because she'd never really had one.

"Dearheart, you need to be presentable. It's not like you're asking the warlock next door to borrow a cup of frog toes," pointed out Gretta. "You're requesting serious magical help."

"That's right." Dretta put her bony hands on her wizened hips. "In our day, you couldn't slap on a pair of jeans and a T-shirt and expect to be granted an audience with a powerful magicker. And Lucas Dark isn't any ol' warlock, either. In fact, I'm not sure he's even a warlock at all."

"I'm aware," said Peace. After all, Zerina made it clear the necromancer was dangerous. Lucas Dark was born and raised in the underworld and had just recently taken up residence on the earthly plane in the new town of Lost Souls & Broken Hearts, Arkansas. So, yeah. He was probably really dangerous. Good. Peace thought dangerous was exactly what she needed if she expected to get rid of Aunt Eartha's hex.

"Are you going to put on lipstick?" Dretta's gaze narrowed. "Or at least some lip balm?"

"Nope."

Peace felt a pinch of guilt, but pushed it deep down where her grief waited for the inevitable. If she did manage to escape Eartha's cruel hex, Peace would have to learn to live without these loving, yet crazy, women who'd saved her and raised her as if she were their own. Maybe if Lucas could fix her situation, he could help her godmothers, too. But…was it really fair to keep them around just so she didn't have to be alone?

She tucked her wallet into her purse and heaved the strap over her shoulder. "C'mon. We gotta see a necromancer about a death hex."

"Are you sure about this?" Gretta offered a smile that revealed yellowed teeth and drew attention to the gash by the right side of her mouth.

Tretta harrumphed and crossed her arms. "Lucas Dark doesn't exactly have a great reputation, either."

"What reputation?" asked Peace.

"Selma Woodhouse told me he was born in the Underworld. The *Underworld*, Peace," repeated Tretta. "You don't mess with the afterlife."

"I already know that," said Peace patiently. "It doesn't change anything."

"Why are you listening to Selma? She's a busybody," said Gretta.

"That's why she always has the good gossip," said Dretta. "And she's the only one willing to do our hair."

"Enough already!" Gretta flung her arm up in the air. Her hand detached and sailed over Peace's head, landing on the bedroom floor. "Selma can't know jack poopy about Lucas Dark. He lives in Lost Souls, and that place is brand-spanking new."

The white and black barking mop AKA Shameless the Shih Tzu skidded across the freshly waxed wood and grabbed the grayish-green hand.

"Shameless! No!" Peace scooped up the shaggy and enthusiastic dog, trying to pry Dretta's thumb out of his growling mouth. Shameless clamped his tiny teeth into the decrepit skin. "Let go. G-Mom needs her hand back. It's the one she uses to show her exasperation."

"Not true," said Gretta. "I use both of my hands." She shuffled across the floor and peered at the dog. "Let go, you overgrown Swiffer!"

Peace rolled her eyes. This was her life. Body parts flying everywhere. Dead godmothers bossing her around. Adorable pet dog getting into trouble. Her actual animal familiar, a persnickety milk snake named Elspeth, napped in Peace's purse, which had a magical pocket created just for Ms. Picky. The only drama Elsa liked came from her favorite soap opera, *The Familiar Way*, an overacted drama that featured a rich raccoon familiar family with their hooks into the small town of Spellsworth.

"How about a treat?" Peace asked Shameless.

The dog paused his thumb gnawing and tilted his head.

"That's right, good boy. Let go of G-Mom's hand, and you'll get a treat."

Shameless immediately released Gretta's thumb and Peace gave her godmother the no-worse-for-wear hand. "We need to duct tape that. It keeps falling off."

"I'll get the Superglue," said Tretta. "I need to reattach some toes anyway."

While the sisters attended to reattaching their body parts, Peace carried her dog down the hallway and into the kitchen. Her ranch style two-bedroom house was small, but cozy—even with three zombies shambling around all the time.

Putting Shameless down, she opened the pantry and withdrew the organic peanut butter dog biscuits. Extracting one from the box, she gave the bone-shaped cookie to him. He trotted off to savor his snack.

As she returned the dog biscuits to the pantry, she guiltily glanced at the door that led to her garage.

I could make a run for it.

Nope. She squashed the urge to zap herself to Mr. Dark's house. It might make explaining why she needed his assistance a whole lot easier if her godmothers weren't there to "help."

Peace heaved a sigh. Alas, she couldn't ditch her caretakers. After all, they'd given up their bodies so she could live. Especially, since she would be losing them all too soon. Stupid, Evil Aunt Eartha.

"Some people are too rotten to live," Peace muttered.

"That's not nice," said Dretta as she and her sisters shuffled into the kitchen. "I know we're rotting, but—"

"I said rotten, not rotting."

Tretta sniffed her underarms. "Now wait a minute. I already have ten layers of deodorant on."

"And a gallon of White Diamonds," said Dretta waving her hand under nose. "You smell like hot garbage anyway."

"You should talk. You put air fresheners in your panties."

"What's wrong with that?"

"Pine scented cardboards tucked in your ass crack makes you smell like fresh squirrel shit."

"You are rotten to the core!" yelled Dretta.

"What? Did you say I'm rotting to my sores?" Gretta said.

"No, damn it. That doesn't even make any sense. Did you lose your ear again?" Dretta glanced at her sister's head. "You need hearing aids."

"You need to change out your air fresheners." Tretta snickered.

"You need to shut up."

"Everyone needs shut up or I'll Superglue your lips shut. Get in the car," instructed Peace. With everyone in the SUV it would be easier to translocate everyone. They'd already arranged with the guardians of Lost Souls, Arkansas to visit. It was also the new home for Zerina. Peace actually felt sorry for Lost Souls. Zerina was a pain in the ass. Still...they hadn't exactly told the necromancer that they were coming. Better to beg forgiveness than ask permission, right?

It took twenty minutes to arrange Dretta, Gretta, and Tretta into the SUV. With Elspeth snuggled into her purse and Shameless on Dretta's lap, Peace was finally able to mutter the location spell.

They instantly appeared in the tiny downtown of Lost Souls, Arkansas.

Zerina had filled her in about the town. The teeny tiny community was made up of mostly witches and shifters, along with vampires, fairies, and the occasional demon. Even so, less than a hundred people lived in the area—all protected by Grace Standing Bear. Apparently, she wielded the ancient magic that used to be a tree, but the power had transferred to Grace, who was wife of the town's bear shifter guardian, Tabor.

Peace had never been to Lost Souls before, but she'd lived in Broken Heart for the last ten years. She was part-fairy, part-witch. Her fairy magic messed with her witch magic, thus having to seek the services of Zerina when she'd fallen down the stupid stairs.

She had some witchery prowess, but her fairy magic was somewhat muted, and Peace didn't rely on her magical attributes for work. Instead, she supported herself by creating crochet items—hats, dolls, blankets, and so forth.

Crochet was rather old-fashioned, but her godmothers had taught her the yarn arts and shown her how to weave in her fairy magic. You didn't just get a hat—you got a hat that changed colors based on your moods. Or gloves that automatically warmed your hands when it got cold outside. Or amigurumi dolls that danced.

Hmm. Downtown was empty. Other than *Fashion by Zerina* (oh goddess help this town) and *Southern Sweets Cafe*, the other buildings were empty. She spotted a small, stand-alone shop on the corner of Main Street and Deliverance Way. The building was painted dark purple and in gold scroll on its only front window was: *Greengrass Tea & Herbal Magic*. None of the business were opened, and no one seemed to be around. In fact, her car was the only one at the four-way stop.

"Zerina said you take Deliverance Way to Styx Road," said Tretta. "You gotta go right, honey."

Zerina had also told them that Lucas Dark lived way off Styx Road in an isolated cabin deep in the forest that surrounded the paranormal town.

Peace was taking a considerable risk by showing up at his door. However, asking the necromancer for help was her last ditch effort. If she didn't figure out a way to rid herself of Aunt Eartha's vicious hex, then in two weeks, Peace would be dead.

And that would suck.

Get your copy of Peace in the Valley!

CHAPTER 1

Lost Souls, Arkansas

*L*ucas Dark slipped through the tall gates made up of blackened and gnarled bones—and raced across the obsidian sand toward the gleaming silver water of the River Styx.

The Underworld had its own devastating beauty, one he'd admired as a child growing up on the banks of Styx. Even now, the stark splendor was breathtaking. He'd never been afraid of his birthplace, despite its terrifying reputation among mortals.

But now ... the fear grew in him like cold slithering vines, squeezing his heart and his lungs.

I'm not too late.

I'm not too late.

As he drew closer to the barren shore, he saw his father Charon help the beautiful redhead into the bone-white gondola.

"Dad!" he screamed.

Charon, dressed in gray robes, a cowled hood drawn over to hide his face, shook his head.

"*No! Stop!*"

The woman looked over her shoulder, her expression one of sad resolve. That desolation struck him to the core. She turned her back toward him and sat down, facing the argent water. He knew they would not cross to the other side to the entrance of the Elysian Fields. No. They would head downstream, toward the tributary that led to the River Hypnos. There, she would wander the shore with no memory of who she was or the life she had lived. Or of him.

I'm not too late.

Lucas realized he'd been running as fast as he could, but now he was stuck in one place, feet digging into the hot silt, chest heaving with exertion.

His father used the oar to push the creaking boat away from the shore.

Lucas opened his mouth to scream his protest, yet no words issued forth.

Pinned into place, helpless, he watched his father direct the boat down the river—taking away the other half of his soul.

~

$\mathcal{L}$ucas bolted upright, drenched in sweat. He took several steady breaths and attempted to calm the frantic beating of his heart.

For the last seven nights he dreamed of the redhead with the gold-green eyes and the sad expression. He pressed his fingers against his temples, frustration curling through him. Dream portents were not his specialty and all attempts to figure out the meaning of the nightmare had proven inadequate.

He felt connected to the woman. Like … like she really was his other half. Lucas rubbed a hand through his short black hair. How was it possible to know someone he'd never met? Hell, who probably didn't even exist except in his imagination?

Maybe he needed a consultation with his mother. Her gentle manner and caring nature was nearly always soothing. That unique kindness was part of her healing gift. She was the opposite of Dad. Charon tended to be brusque and no-nonsense with mortals and immortals alike. Dad needed Mom's softness, her sweet benevolence to counter his practical nature and rough edges.

Lucas shook off his thoughts. Not for the first time he wished he could call Mom on a cell phone. Technology didn't work in the Underworld—not that anyone would want to put cell towers on the silty shores of the River Styx. Dad would hate that. Besides, Cerberus would just knock them over and gnaw on 'em like chewies.

Sighing, Lucas lay back down and pulled the covers up to his chin. But no matter how much he tried, he couldn't go back to sleep.

And he couldn't forget about the mystery woman who haunted his waking hours, too.

Was she real?

~

Broken Heart, Oklahoma

"*Y*ou should wear a dress." Dretta's rheumy blue gaze appraised Peace Crawford's jeans and the navy-blue T-shirt emblazoned with "I crochet so I don't kill people." She frowned as she studied Peace's bright green Converses. "Why do you insist on wearing those shoes?"

"Because they're comfortable. And not high heels." Peace

pulled her wavy red hair into a ponytail and whispered a spell to keep it that way. "Let's not forget the sad tale of the Heels of Regret." Peace spread out her hands. "A cocktail party. A marble staircase. And the stilettos from hell."

"Well, it's not like you had to walk around with that broken ankle. Zerina fixed that right up for you," said Dretta.

Peace remembered her emergency trip to Zerina's house. Ugh. Still, she had the fairy to thank for sending her Lucas Dark's direction. It was Zerina's suggestion that the necromancer might be able to help.

"Now there's a fairy who knows fashion. You could ask her for some tips," said Dretta.

"No way. Don't you remember? She laughed the entire time she healed my ankle. And then she stole my heels. That woman has a serious addiction to Prada."

"Forget about the shoes." Tretta she shuffled around her sister. She only had one eye and wore a sparkly blue eyepatch over the other desiccated socket. "What you need is a leisure suit. Red plaid with a white belt."

"She's not going to a 1970s disco." Gretta pushed her way between her sisters and pointed a gnarled gray finger at her godchild. "Ignore them. They wouldn't know fashion if they tripped over it. What you need, Peace, is low-cut blouse to show off your boobs."

"I'm not changing clothes." Peace loved her zombie godmothers, she really did. But they were not exactly fashion icons. Her godmothers were dressed in tracksuits—Dretta in purple, Tretta in blue, and Gretta in pink. Add to that bright white orthopedic shoes, and you had the opposite of stylish. So, Peace was going to ignore their clothing advice and shelve it right next to their dating advice. Not that she needed opinions about her love life because she'd never really had one.

"Dearheart, you need to be presentable. It's not like you're asking the warlock next door to borrow a cup of frog toes," pointed out Gretta. "You're requesting serious magical help."

"That's right." Dretta put her bony hands on her wizened hips. "In our day, you couldn't slap on a pair of jeans and a T-shirt and expect to be granted an audience with a powerful magicker. And Lucas Dark isn't any ol' warlock, either. In fact, I'm not sure he's even a warlock at all."

"I'm aware," said Peace. After all, Zerina made it clear the necromancer was dangerous. Lucas Dark was born and raised in the underworld and had just recently taken up residence on the earthly plane in the new town of Lost Souls & Broken Hearts, Arkansas. So, yeah. He was probably really dangerous. Good. Peace thought dangerous was exactly what she needed if she expected to get rid of Aunt Eartha's hex.

"Are you going to put on lipstick?" Dretta's gaze narrowed. "Or at least some lip balm?"

"Nope."

Peace felt a pinch of guilt, but pushed it deep down where her grief waited for the inevitable. If she did manage to escape Eartha's cruel hex, Peace would have to learn to live without these loving, yet crazy, women who'd saved her and raised her as if she were their own. Maybe if Lucas could fix her situation, he could help her godmothers, too. But…was it really fair to keep them around just so she didn't have to be alone?

She tucked her wallet into her purse and heaved the strap over her shoulder. "C'mon. We gotta see a necromancer about a death hex."

"Are you sure about this?" Gretta offered a smile that revealed yellowed teeth and drew attention to the gash by the right side of her mouth.

Tretta harrumphed and crossed her arms. "Lucas Dark doesn't exactly have a great reputation, either."

"What reputation?" asked Peace.

"Selma Woodhouse told me he was born in the Underworld. The *Underworld*, Peace," repeated Tretta. "You don't mess with the afterlife."

"I already know that," said Peace patiently. "It doesn't change anything."

"Why are you listening to Selma? She's a busybody," said Gretta.

"That's why she always has the good gossip," said Dretta. "And she's the only one willing to do our hair."

"Enough already!" Gretta flung her arm up in the air. Her hand detached and sailed over Peace's head, landing on the bedroom floor. "Selma can't know jack poopy about Lucas Dark. He lives in Lost Souls, and that place is brand-spanking new."

The white and black barking mop AKA Shameless the Shih Tzu skidded across the freshly waxed wood and grabbed the grayish-green hand.

"Shameless! No!" Peace scooped up the shaggy and enthusiastic dog, trying to pry Dretta's thumb out of his growling mouth. Shameless clamped his tiny teeth into the decrepit skin. "Let go. G-Mom needs her hand back. It's the one she uses to show her exasperation."

"Not true," said Gretta. "I use both of my hands." She shuffled across the floor and peered at the dog. "Let go, you overgrown Swiffer!"

Peace rolled her eyes. This was her life. Body parts flying everywhere. Dead godmothers bossing her around. Adorable pet dog getting into trouble. Her actual animal familiar, a persnickety milk snake named Elspeth, napped in Peace's purse, which had a magical pocket created just for Ms. Picky. The only drama Elsa liked came from her favorite soap opera, *The Familiar Way*, an overacted drama that featured a rich raccoon familiar family with their hooks into the small town of Spellsworth.

"How about a treat?" Peace asked Shameless.

The dog paused his thumb gnawing and tilted his head.

"That's right, good boy. Let go of G-Mom's hand, and you'll get a treat."

Shameless immediately released Gretta's thumb and Peace gave her godmother the no-worse-for-wear hand. "We need to duct tape that. It keeps falling off."

"I'll get the Superglue," said Tretta. "I need to reattach some toes anyway."

While the sisters attended to reattaching their body parts, Peace carried her dog down the hallway and into the kitchen. Her ranch style two-bedroom house was small, but cozy—even with three zombies shambling around all the time.

Putting Shameless down, she opened the pantry and withdrew the organic peanut butter dog biscuits. Extracting one from the box, she gave the bone-shaped cookie to him. He trotted off to savor his snack.

As she returned the dog biscuits to the pantry, she guiltily glanced at the door that led to her garage.

I could make a run for it.

Nope. She squashed the urge to zap herself to Mr. Dark's house. It might make explaining why she needed his assistance a whole lot easier if her godmothers weren't there to "help."

Peace heaved a sigh. Alas, she couldn't ditch her caretakers. After all, they'd given up their bodies so she could live. Especially, since she would be losing them all too soon. Stupid, Evil Aunt Eartha.

"Some people are too rotten to live," Peace muttered.

"That's not nice," said Dretta as she and her sisters shuffled into the kitchen. "I know we're rotting, but—"

"I said rotten, not rotting."

Tretta sniffed her underarms. "Now wait a minute. I already have ten layers of deodorant on."

MICHELE BARDSLEY

"And a gallon of White Diamonds," said Dretta waving her hand under nose. "You smell like hot garbage anyway."

"You should talk. You put air fresheners in your panties."

"What's wrong with that?"

"Pine scented cardboards tucked in your ass crack makes you smell like fresh squirrel shit."

"You are rotten to the core!" yelled Dretta.

"What? Did you say I'm rotting to my sores?" Gretta said.

"No, damn it. That doesn't even make any sense. Did you lose your ear again?" Dretta glanced at her sister's head. "You need hearing aids."

"You need to change out your air fresheners." Tretta snickered.

"You need to shut up."

"Everyone needs shut up or I'll Superglue your lips shut. Get in the car," instructed Peace. With everyone in the SUV it would be easier to translocate everyone. They'd already arranged with the guardians of Lost Souls, Arkansas to visit. It was also the new home for Zerina. Peace actually felt sorry for Lost Souls. Zerina was a pain in the ass. Still…they hadn't exactly told the necromancer that they were coming. Better to beg forgiveness than ask permission, right?

It took twenty minutes to arrange Dretta, Gretta, and Tretta into the SUV. With Elspeth snuggled into her purse and Shameless on Dretta's lap, Peace was finally able to mutter the location spell.

They instantly appeared in the tiny downtown of Lost Souls, Arkansas.

Zerina had filled her in about the town. The teeny tiny community was made up of mostly witches and shifters, along with vampires, fairies, and the occasional demon. Even so, less than a hundred people lived in the area—all protected by Grace Standing Bear. Apparently, she wielded the ancient magic that used to be a tree, but the power had transferred to Grace, who was wife of the town's bear shifter guardian, Tabor.

Peace had never been to Lost Souls before, but she'd lived in Broken Heart for the last ten years. She was part-fairy, part-witch. Her fairy magic messed with her witch magic, thus having to seek the services of Zerina when she'd fallen down the stupid stairs.

She had some witchery prowess, but her fairy magic was somewhat muted, and Peace didn't rely on her magical attributes for work. Instead, she supported herself by creating crochet items—hats, dolls, blankets, and so forth.

Crochet was rather old-fashioned, but her godmothers had taught her the yarn arts and shown her how to weave in her fairy magic. You didn't just get a hat—you got a hat that changed colors based on your moods. Or gloves that automatically warmed your hands when it got cold outside. Or amigurumi dolls that danced.

Hmm. Downtown was empty. Other than *Fashion by Zerina* (oh goddess help this town) and *Southern Sweets Cafe,* the other buildings were empty. She spotted a small, stand-alone shop on the corner of Main Street and Deliverance Way. The building was painted dark purple and in gold scroll on its only front window was: *Greengrass Tea & Herbal Magic.* None of the business were opened, and no one seemed to be around. In fact, her car was the only one at the four-way stop.

"Zerina said you take Deliverance Way to Styx Road," said Tretta. "You gotta go right, honey."

Zerina had also told them that Lucas Dark lived way off Styx Road in an isolated cabin deep in the forest that surrounded the paranormal town.

Peace was taking a considerable risk by showing up at his

door. However, asking the necromancer for help was her last ditch effort. If she didn't figure out a way to rid herself of Aunt Eartha's vicious hex, then in two weeks, Peace would be dead.

And that would suck.

ROMANCES BY MICHELE BARDSLEY

Broken Heart Paranormal Romances

#1 - I'm the Vampire, That's Why

#2 - Don't Talk Back to Your Vampire

#3 - Because Your Vampire Said So

#4 - Wait Till Your Vampire Gets Home

#5 - Over My Dead Body

#6 - Come Hell or High Water

#7 - Cross Your Heart

#8 - Must Love Lycans

#9 - Only Lycans Need Apply

#10 - Broken Heart Tails

#11 - Some Lycan Hot

#12 - You'll Understand When You're Dead

#13 - Lycan on the Edge

#14 - Your Lycan or Mine?

Lost Souls & Broken Hearts

A Broken Heart Paranormal Romance Spin-off

#1 - Amazing Grace

#2 - Peace in the Valley

#3 - How Great Thou Art

Wizards of Nevermore Fantasy Romances

#1 - Never Again

#2 - Now or Never

The Pack Rules Shifter Romances

#1 - Alpha

#2 - Wolves

#3 - Bears

#4 - Dragons

#5 - Cats

Single Title Paranormal Romances

Holiday Bites

Blood Kiss

Cursed

Wired

Magical Acts

Tek

Single Title Contemporary Romances

Frisky Business

Mirrors Falls: Daddy in Training and Bride in Training

MYSTERIES BY MICHELE BARDSLEY

Violetta Graves Paranormal Mysteries

The Complete Series

#1 - In Good Spirits

#2 - A Spirited Defense

#3 - Getting in the Spirit

#4 - Plagued by Spirits

#5 - Free Spirit

Graves Detective Agency Cozy Mysteries

#1 - A Grave Mistake (December 2019)

#2 - One Foot in the Grave (April 2019)

#3 - Grave Robber (June 2019)

#4 - Take It to the Grave (October 2019)

#5 - Grave Stone (January 2020)

Broken Heart Paranormal Cozy Mysteries

#1 - Dirty Rotten Vampires (October 2018)

#2 - Twelve Angry Vampires (January 2019)

#3 - Citizen Vampire (April 2019)

#4 - The Vampire Connection (August 2019)

#5 - A Vampire in Paris (October 2019)

Garden Grove Witches of the Northwest

#1 - A Witch in Thyme (November 2018)

#2 - Stop and Spell the Roses (February 2019)

ABOUT THE AUTHOR

Michele Bardsley is a *New York Times* and *USA Today* best-selling author of paranormal fiction. When she's not writing tales of otherworldly adventures, she watches "Supernatural," consumes chocolate, crochets hats, reads voraciously, and spends time with her Viking hubby and their fur babies.

Visit Michele's Website
http://www.michelebardsley.com

Subscribe to Michele's Newsletter
http://www.michelebardsleynewsletter.com

f facebook.com/MicheleBardsleyNovels

BB bookbub.com/authors/michele-bardsley

g goodreads.com/michelebardsley

a amazon.com/author/michelebardsley